LEGENDS OF THE
N⬤RSE KINGS

Illustrations by Everett Kintsler

This edition published by Floris Books in 2013

 This book is also available
as an eBook

British Library CIP Data available
ISBN 978-086315-942-8

Printed in Great Britain
by Page Bros Ltd.

LEGENDS OF THE
N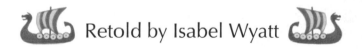RSE KINGS

THE SAGA OF KING RAGNAR GOATSKIN
AND THE DREAM OF KING ALFDAN

Retold by Isabel Wyatt

Floris Books

The Saga of King Ragnar Goatskin

An Old Danish Hero Tale

CONTENTS

1. TORA HART IS BORN

In the days of Sigurd the Dragon Slayer, King Herrad was King of Gothland. His hall stood on a tall cliff above his harbour. Each spring, when the corn had been sown, he went out with his longships on a Viking raid. Each midsummer he came back to reap the ripe corn. When the corn was safe in the cornlofts, away he went again, to raid till winter gales drove him home. From this he got his nickname of Herrad Sea-Rover.

One Midsummer Day, the lookout on the roof blew his horn. He blew King Herrad's special note. In the hall the glad news flew from lip to lip: "King Herrad Sea-Rover is back!"

The longships sailed into the harbour under the cliff. The servants ran down the cliff path from the hall, to pull the ships up on to the beach. Kalf, King Herrad's wise advisor, stood at the edge of the sea to call his news to the king: "Lord, this very day a child has been born to you!"

King Herrad sprang onto the land. He strode up the beach with Kalf, the Wiseman. The sun glinted off the gold of his helmet and chain mail. He strode across the rye fields to his hall, and then up the hall to his high seat. Servants ran to bring him wine in a golden wine cup. A servant girl stood with a silver bowl of hot water, to wash his hands and feet.

But King Herrad cried, "First, I want to see my child!"

Queen Hild's maidservants swept down the stone stairs from her private bedroom. They laid the baby naked at the feet of the king.

"But it is a girl!" cried King Herrad. "My wish was for a son."

Kalf the Wiseman shook his head. He was wise beyond most men, for he saw things that were to come.

"This baby wouldn't have been a strong son," he said. "But the son-in-law she will give you will be the best of men."

King Herrad was pleased to hear this. "Let the child live, then," he said. "I give her the name 'Tora.'"

"She will be known as Tora Hart," Kalf told him. "In the same way the hart is more noble than other animals, Tora Hart will be more fair and wise than other girls."

"Bright thread and dark thread are woven in each person's web of fate," said King Herrad. "What can you see of the bright and the dark in this child's web of fate?"

And Kalf told him, "Her life will not be long, but she will live it well loved by all. It will be a happy life, once she is married."

"And till then?" asked King Herrad.

"I see a time," Kalf told him, "when she'll be known not as Tora Hart, but as Tora Hart-in-the-Tower. During that time she will not be free."

"Can I do anything to stop it?" asked King Herrad.

"It is you who will cause it," Kalf told him. "It is your earth-ready gift to her that will make this happen." In those days, when a girl was fourteen years old, she was said to be earth-ready, and her father gave her an earth-ready gift.

"Then she shall get no earth-ready gift from me," cried King Herrad.

But Kalf the Wiseman said, "If a fate is meant to be, it will be, whatever you do. And dark thread and light thread lie so close together in her web of fate that it is out of this very web that your son-in-law will come."

Then Queen Hild's maidservants took the newborn baby away. The servant girls came with fresh water, to wash King Herrad's hands and feet.

He drank his wine. Then he strode out of the hall, and up the stone steps, to greet Queen Hild in her private bedroom.

2. THE GOLDEN EGG AND THE SILVER EGG

Seven years went by. The time came for Tora Hart's tooth gift. In those days, when children lost their first milktooth, their mother gave them a tooth gift.

The tooth gift Queen Hild gave to Tora Hart was a golden egg.

"How can I hatch it, Mother?" asked Tora Hart.

"Set it in the sun's rays, my child," said Queen Hild.

"What will hatch out of it, Mother?" asked Tora Hart.

"In three days, you will see," said Queen Hild, with a smile.

So Tora Hart put the golden egg on the window seat in her mother's room. For three days it lay in the sun's rays.

The next day Tora Hart saw a crack in the golden shell. The shell fell in two and out came a small, snow-white swan. As Tora Hart grew, the white swan grew, and where Tora Hart went, the white swan went too. From the day the white swan was born, it never left her side.

And now Queen Hild began to teach Tora Hart how to lay gold thread on scarlet cloth; how to spin flax so strong that it rang like a harp string; how to weave webs so fine that they went into a finger ring; how to grow herbs, and make ointments from them, and look after people who were sick, and heal injuries.

And Kalf the Wiseman began to teach Tora Hart magical songs, and starcraft, and the art of speech, and how to play chess, and how to sing old ballads, and how to make new ones.

And seven more years went by.

Then Kalf the Wiseman said to King Herrad, "The princess will soon be earth-ready. Then for a time Tora Hart must be Tora Hart-in-the-Tower. That tower will be her home till she is free. So make it comfortable for her, and stock it well with food and wine."

King Herrad agreed with Kalf the Wiseman and he made a home for Tora Hart in a tall tower. It had a golden roof ridge, and it had a well inside. He put in it good store of food and wine. He put in a big window over a beautiful window seat. Looking one way Tora Hart could see the sea and the harbour at the foot of the cliff; the other way, she saw the corn fields beyond the gate of her tower.

Spring came, and the time to sow seed. King Herrad had rye seed sown in the fields next to his hall, and barley around Tora Hart's tower. Then he took his men and his longships, and set sail on his spring raids.

Summer came. The barley was tall and green all round Tora Hart's tower when one day the lookout blew King Herrad's special note from the roof of the hall. It was Midsummer Day again; on that day, Tora Hart was fourteen years old.

She ran to her window, to look out to sea.

Far out she saw a fleet of ships, with dragon prows high above the waves, and sails striped blue and white, and glint after glint from the shields that hung along the sides of each ship.

Tora Hart ran down from her tower, her white swan at her side. Queen Hild ran down from her room in her tall headdress. They took hands and ran between green barley and green rye, down the steep cliff path, and over the white sand to the white foam at the edge of the sea.

The servants and maidservants came in a happy crowd after them. They stood on the beach, to welcome King Herrad Sea-Rover home.

King Herrad sprang onto the land. He flung one arm around the queen, and one around the princess. Then the three of them went up the beach and up the cliff and into his hall.

From the longships, the shipmen flung onto land the items they'd gathered in that spring's raids. The servants carried it all up the cliff to the hall, and laid it out on benches and tables. Then everyone went round the hall to gaze at it – arm rings of gold, cups decorated with gems, necklaces of amber, swords with golden hilts, silver harnesses, helmets with crests of gold, rich robes, gold cloth and scarlet silks.

King Herrad gave a gift to each person out of his share of the plunder. He asked Tora Hart, "What gift would you like, daughter?"

"This, Father," she said. And she picked up a small silver egg.

"That is a small gift for a princess," he said. "But take it, with my good wishes."

He didn't remember that it was Tora Hart's birthday, and that today she was fourteen years old. And so it came to pass that he gave her an earth-ready gift, after all.

3. Tora's Dragon Is Born

Tora Hart asked her white swan, "How shall I hatch my silver egg, white swan?"

"Set it under my wing," said her white swan.

Tora Hart asked her white swan, "What will hatch out of it, white swan?"

"In six days you will see," said her white swan.

For three days the white swan sat with the silver egg under her wing. Then she said, "The moon is full, Tora Hart. For the next three nights, set the egg in the moon's rays."

So Tora Hart put the silver egg on her window seat. For the next three nights it lay in the moon's rays. And the next day Tora Hart saw a crack in the silver shell. Then the silver shell fell in two and Tora Hart saw a tiny green snake glide out, as small as her own little finger.

It was so like a toy that she picked it up with glee, and ran to show it to King Herrad. King Herrad sat with Queen Hild on the high seat in his hall.

"Look, Father!" cried Tora Hart. "A tiny dragon has come out of your silver egg, like the dragons that lie on gold."

King Herrad said with a smile, "Let this one lie on gold, then." And he pulled a ring off his finger, and gave it to her.

"If it is a true dragon," said Tora Hart, "the gold will grow as the dragon grows."

And King Herrad joked with her, "Then the gold shall go with you as a wedding gift when you marry, daughter."

"Your little dragon will need a little lair, my child," said Queen Hild. "I will give you a little glass casket for it to lie in, on its gold." And she sent one of her servant girls to her room, to fetch the little glass casket.

Tora Hart put King Herrad's ring in the little glass casket and then she let the tiny green snake glide in and coil on it.

When she went to bed that night, she put the little glass casket on her window seat. All that night, the moon's rays fed the snake. And all that night, the snake fed the gold.

When Tora Hart woke up the next day, she saw that the ring had grown as big as an arm ring. The tiny green snake had grown as big as an arm ring, too.

She ran to show her father and mother the little glass casket. They thought it was very funny. Queen Hild said, "This lair will soon be too small for your little dragon, my child. So tonight it shall sleep in your old cradle." So Queen Hild sent two servant girls to put Tora Hart's cradle in Tora Hart's room.

Tora Hart put the golden arm ring in the cradle; then she let the green snake glide in and coil on it.

When she went to bed that night, she put the cradle in the moon's rays by her window seat. All that night, the moon's rays fed the snake. And all that night, the snake fed the gold.

When Tora Hart woke up the next day, she saw that the golden arm ring was now as big as a giant's, and the green snake was as thick as her father's arm.

King Herrad joked with her, "You didn't grow as fast when you lay in that cradle, daughter!"

Queen Hild said, "I must find you a chest for your dragon's next lair, my child." She sent four servants to take a big chest from her own room to Tora Hart's. And in this the green snake slept that night, on its giant arm ring of gold.

All that night, the moon's rays fed the snake. And all that night, the snake fed the gold.

When Tora Hart woke up the next day, she saw that the golden arm ring now came up to the top of the chest, forcing the lid open. The snake lay on top of the big hoop of gold. The snake was now as thick as King Herrad's body. A crest had grown along its back, and its head was as high as the ceiling.

"It has grown too big to be kept in your room, my child," said Queen Hild. "You must keep it out of doors." So she sent six servants to drag the chest, full of gold, down from Tora Hart's room in the tower. At the gate, they took out the hoop of gold, and it slid round the tower till a ring of gold lay all around it.

The green snake slid down the steps after them, and lay on the gold, and slept. All that night, the moon's rays fed the snake. And all that night, the snake fed the gold.

When Tora Hart woke up the next day, she rose and ran to her window. She saw a wall of gold all round her tower. On it lay a full-grown dragon, its skin thick with iron scales.

Tora Hart ran down from her tower, to go to tell her father. But when she came to the tower gate, the dragon lay in her way.

"You may not leave, Tora Hart," it said, "as long as I keep watch and guard over you."

Then the servants ran out from King Herrad's hall to see the dragon. It lay so still, with such a mild look on its face, that they got sticks and began to prod it. At that the dragon let out a loud roar, and spurts of smoke and venom came from its mouth. The servants fell back in such fear that they trod the barley flat.

"No one may enter the princess's tower," the dragon cried out, "as long as I keep watch and guard over her. No one may enter; and no one may leave."

And this was how Tora Hart became Tora Hart-in-the-Tower.

4. KALF MAKES A MAGIC MIRROR

At that first roar of Tora Hart's dragon, King Herrad sprang up and strode to the door of his hall. Kalf the Wiseman went with him.

At the sight that met his eyes, the king stood as still as stone. "Look, it will not let her out, nor the servants in!" he cried. "How will she and her servants manage?"

"You have put a store of food and wine in her tower," said Kalf. "They will live on that till we find a hero to slay the dragon and set her free."

"We will send for Sigurd the Dragon Slayer," said King Herrad. "He shall marry Tora Hart-in-the-Tower, and take the dragon gold as a wedding gift."

"Sigurd went south, into the Land of the Niflungs, the Men of the Mist," said Kalf, "and a thick mist hides his fate from me. He may not be free to marry our Tora Hart-in-the Tower."

"But you told me on her birth night that she was to marry the first and best of men," cried King Herrad. "Is that not Sigurd?"

"It is," said Kalf. "I will catch the image of the princess in a magic mirror, and go and seek him with it." So Kalf made a magic mirror, and over it he said special verses of power.

He went across from the hall to the tower gate. The crest rose along the dragon's back. It gave a snort, and smoke came in puffs from its mouth. It cried with a roar, "No one may enter the tower while I keep watch and guard over her!"

"Be still, Dragon!" said Kalf. "I only want to see her." And he called to her, "Hello, Tora Hart-in-the-Tower!"

Tora came to the window of her tower. She was dressed in white linen, with her high royal head-dress on her long golden hair. She sat on her window seat like a swan on a still wave, as white as the white swan at her side.

She sat full in the sun's rays. Kalf the Wiseman held up his magic mirror, and her image was reflected on its glass.

"Keep your spirits up, Tora Hart-in-the-Tower," said Kalf. "I will go to find a hero to slay this dragon and set you free."

At this, the dragon gave a roar that shook the wall of gold he lay on. Kalf hid his magic mirror in his cloak, took his horse, and set off to seek for Sigurd.

He rode south by long roads, till he came at last to Mirkwood. Along its dark forest paths he rode, till he came to where four roads met. He saw a man ride swift as the wind from the south side of the wood. At the crossroads, the man slowed to look around him, and Kalf saw the white foam of speed on his horse's sides.

When he saw Kalf, the man cried, "I'm lucky to meet you, a friendly stranger! I'm lost. Tell me, have you ridden from Lymdale?"

"No, friend, from Gothland," Kalf told him.

"Then this path to my right will be my way to Lymdale," said the stranger. And he turned his horse that way.

"Stay," said Kalf. "You ride from the Land of the Niflungs. Is Sigurd the Dragon Slayer there?"

The man reined in his horse so quickly that he made his horse rear up.

"Sigurd is dead," he said. "That is why I'm riding in such haste to Lymdale."

"Dead?" cried Kalf; and the mist in his mind grew clear, and he knew that this was true. "Who did such a terrible thing?"

"Hogni, his own bloodbrother," the stranger told him. "I saw it between the trees as I gave my horse water at a brook. Sigurd was lying flat, to drink at a spring, and Hogni drove his spear into the red cross on Sigurd's back."

"But why does that send you in haste to Lymdale?" Kalf asked.

"When Hogni had killed him, he said to those with him, 'The tree is dead; let no branch of it live.' Then I remembered that Sigurd left his child, Asla, with King Himir of Lymdale. And so I'm riding to warn him."

"Sigurd was the first and best of men," said Kalf. "Who is left who can take his place?"

"Men say Ragnar, King of Denmark, is good prospect," said the stranger. "He is only fifteen years old, but he is big and mighty. If you're seeking a hero for a great deed, seek Ragnar. This fourth road leads to Denmark."

"I thank you, friend. Speed well on your errand," said Kalf.

The stranger spurred on his horse, and took the road to Lymdale. Kalf sat still, to look into his mind. In it he saw a face, not yet that of a man, but strong and bold, with red hair held back by a golden headband.

"Then that is why a mist hid Sigurd in my mind," said Kalf. "I will go and find King Ragnar. If he looks like this, I shall know he is the hero I seek."

And he, too, spurred on his horse, and took the road to Denmark.

5. Ragnar Sees Tora In The Magic Mirror

Kalf came at last to Ledra, on the Danish coast. The King of Denmark had his hall here. He found King Ragnar's lords in the field, in a trial of skill. He reined in his horse to watch.

Kalf saw that one of the crowd was best at all things – when they threw a spear, when they swung a sword, when they bent a bow. His face was not yet that of a man, but his frame was big and strong and fit for manly deeds. Under his helmet, his hair was red.

"Ragnar! Ragnar! Ragnar!" the crowd of servants cried, at each fresh feat of arms.

When the trials of skill were over, Kalf went over to him. Then he saw that the face of King Ragnar was the face he had seen in his mind's eye at the crossroads in Mirkwood. "Lord, my name is Kalf. I am advisor to Herrad Sea-Rover, King of Gothland. He sent me to you, with a thing for you to see." He took his magic mirror from the folds of his cloak and held it up, before King Ragnar's eyes.

In the mirror, King Ragnar saw the image of Tora Hart-in-the-Tower, dressed in her white linen robe and her long golden hair. She sat on her window seat like a swan on a still wave, as white as the white swan at her side.

King Ragnar held his breath. Then he cried, "She's the loveliest woman I've ever seen. She is as white and bright as the brightest day."

"She is a golden girl," agreed Kalf. "And with her will go a great store of dragon's gold." He told King Ragnar the tale of Tora's dragon. King Ragnar's eyes were still on the white and golden image in the magic mirror. "Just seeing her image makes my heart glad," he cried. "Stay here with me tonight. Then ride back and tell King Herrad that in three days I shall be on my way by sea, to fight the dragon."

So Kalf spent that night with King Ragnar at Ledra. And next day he set out to ride back to Gothland.

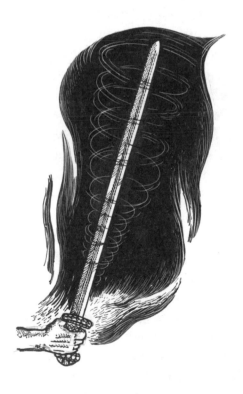

The watchman on the roof-ridge blew Kalf's note on his horn when he saw Kalf ride up the steep cliff path. At once King Herrad and Queen Hild came swiftly out from the hall, to meet him and to hear his news.

Queen Hild asked, with a catch of her breath, "Did you find Sigurd? Is he on his way?"

"Sigurd is no longer of this world," said Kalf. And he told them how Sigurd had been killed.

"There can't be anyone else like Sigurd," said King Herrad. "He was as far above other men as gold is above iron. We set our hopes too high when we set them on Sigurd."

"But the man most like Sigurd in all our Northlands is on his way to fight the dragon," Kalf told them.

"Who is that?" they both asked at once.

"King Ragnar of Denmark," said Kalf.

"King Ragnar?" cried King Herrad. "But he's only a boy."

"In age, yes," said Kalf. "But his frame is as big and strong as a man's. He can wield a sword, throw a spear, shoot a shaft, bend a bow. Soon he will not be bettered in all the Northlands for might, and for clear mind, and for stout heart."

"But does he have a skin of horn, as Sigurd had?" asked King Herrad. "If not, how can he face the dragon's venom?"

"He doesn't have Sigurd's skin of horn," said Kalf. "But he has a mind as quick as his arm is strong. He will find a way, you will see, to face the dragon's venom."

Then Kalf went across from the rye fields, and stood at the edge of the barley, to call across the dragon, up to Tora's room, "Hello, Tora Hart-in-the-Tower!"

Tora came to her window, a girl all white and gold, her white swan at her side.

"Be happy," Kalf cried up to her. "You will not be Tora Hart-in-the-Tower for long. A king is on his way to slay your dragon for you – a strong young king, with red hair."

At this, the dragon gave a roar that shook its bed of gold. And Tora cried to her servants, "We should be happy! A king is on his way to set us free – a strong young king, with red hair!"

6. Ragnar Slays The Dragon

Tora Hart-in-the-Tower sat on her window seat with her servants. They laid gold and silver thread on scarlet cloth. The dragon lay still, coiled all round the tower.

"The dragon sleeps in the sun," said Princess Tora. She rose, to look down at him. Then her eyes went the other way, to the sea. The waves were big and bright. She saw a ship rock over them, with sails of blue and gold. A shield wall, red shield next to white shield, lay close along its sides.

She saw a man standing at the prow of the ship. In the sun, his helmet and his chain mail were as bright as glass. A spear was in his right hand, and on his left arm was a round shield, embossed with gold.

Tora Hart-in-the-Tower held her breath as the ship sailed into the harbour. Soon it was out of sight under the cliff.

King Ragnar's men sprang out into the surf and drew the ship up on the beach. "Lord, you're not going to face the dragon dressed as you are?" they cried.

"No," said King Ragnar. "First I must put on a skin the dragon's venom will not harm, like Sigurd's skin of horn." From the hold of the ship he got a longshirt, a hood, a mask and trousers, all made of goatskin. "Bring me hot tar," he said, and the men lit a fire of driftwood on the beach, to heat the tar.

"Dip the goatskin in the hot tar," said King Ragnar. The men did so.

"Now cover the tar with sand," said King Ragnar. The men did so.

"Now I will put on my skin of horn," said King Ragnar. He took off his helmet and his chain mail. He put on the goatskin longshirt and hood and trousers.

When his men saw him dressed in them, they let out a shout of laughter. "Lord," cried one, "till now you had no nickname. But from this day you shall be known as Ragnar Goatskin!"

And all his men took up the cry, "Ragnar Goatskin! Death to the dragon, and a fair bride for our King Goatskin!"

King Ragnar picked up his shield, his spear and his goatskin hood. "Wait for me here," he said. Then up the beach and up the cliff he went.

He walked between the rows of barley to the gate of Tora's tower. There he found the dragon, fast asleep.

He lifted his head to look at the tower. Tora Hart-in-the-Tower stood at her window, all white and gold, her white swan at her side. King Ragnar pulled off his hood, so that she saw his red hair, held back by a golden headband. He stood in the sun, and sang to her:

> *Tora Hart-in-the-Tower,*
> *Swan white, sun bright,*
> *The dragon guards you now*
> *Within your wall of gold.*
> *Tora Hart-in-the-Tower,*
> *Soon, soon you shall be free!*

Tora bent down from the window to look at him. In his goatskin trousers and longshirt, he could have been a servant. But in his right hand was his spear, and on his left arm was slung his shield, embossed with gold.

Tora Hart-in-the-Tower cried down to him, "Noble stranger, my heart wishes for everything to go well for you!"

King Ragnar pulled on his hood again.

One of the maidservants said to the rest, "He comes at a good time. He can slay the dragon while it is asleep." But Tora Hart-in-the-Tower said, "My heart tells me that even with a dragon, he will fight fair."

She was right, for King Ragnar cried with a loud voice, "Hello, dragon! Wake up!" And he gave the dragon a prod with his spear.

The dragon woke with a roar that shook the ground and made the barley shake. "A servant in furry trousers! Why are you here? Run away, before I rip you bone from bone."

"I was not born to run away," said Ragnar Goatskin, and stood his ground.

Then the dragon began to snort out smoke, and to spout out venom, and to roar again, "Run away, servant, before I drown you in a flood of venom!"

"My death day is not today," said Ragnar Goatskin. "But yours is, dragon!" He stood back, out of reach, till the dragon began to rear up, and to lash out with both head and tail.

On the dragon's back and sides, its scales lay so thick and close that no spear could pierce them. Only the dragon's underside was soft and had no scales. At last King Ragnar saw his chance. He threw his spear into the dragon's soft flesh under the huge head, with its drip of venom. The spear went in deep.

The dragon bit at Goatskin with a clash and snap of fangs. It bit into the gold rim of Goatskin's shield. It began to lash to and fro in its death throes, because Ragnar's spear had pierced its heart.

King Goatskin had to wade in a pool of venom up to his knees as he tried to pull out his spear. But he had driven it too far in. The spear broke and the spearhead was left in the dragon's heart.

Tora Hart-in-the-Tower, still at her window, said, "That was a hero's fight!"

"But he's only a servant," said one of the servant girls. "Look at his goatskin clothes."

"You didn't see him without his hood on," said Tora Hart-in-the-Tower. "I think he's the king that Kalf said was on his way. Fill me a wine cup, so I can drink to him."

Her servants did so, and she held the cup in her hand. But he had gone. After a while, she saw the ship sail out from under the cliff, out to sea. A man in helmet and chain mail as bright as glass stood at the prow.

7. Orm Claims Tora Hart

Tora Hart was now Tora Hart-in-the-Tower no more. She and her servant girls ate that day in her father's hall, and slept that night in her mother's room.

King Herrad sent his men to bring in the dragon's gold, and store it in his chests. "As for the dragon," he said, "we must give it a great mound for a grave. But first let it lie for three days, so that all its venom drains away."

"But who slew the dragon, my child?" asked Queen Hild.

"And where is he now?" asked King Herrad.

"I think it was the king with red hair that Kalf told me about," said Tora Hart. "I saw his ship sail away." But her servant girls said, "It wasn't a king. It was a servant." They talked about his goatskin trousers, and how the dragon had torn a bit of gold from the rim of his shield, and of how his spearhead had been left in the dragon's heart.

This ran from servant to servant, down the hall. Then Orm, one of the servants, said to himself, "I will try to get that spearhead and that bit of shield. Then I can also get the princess and the gold."

Orm was the only one from the King's hall who had seen King Ragnar sail away, and first he had seen him take off his goatskin hood and mask and longshirt and trousers, and put on his chain mail and helmet.

"The dragon will still be full of venom," said Orm. "But in that goatskin, I'll be safe from it." So he crept down the cliff, and found the goatskins on the beach, just as King Ragnar had left them. Orm hid them till night fell. Then he put them on and went out to the huge dragon that lay so still at Tora Hart's tower gate.

By the light of the moon, he crept among the dragon's folds. He felt in the dragon's mouth for the scrap of King Ragnar's shield-rim. He felt in the dragon's heart for the head of King Ragnar's spear. Dressed in King Ragnar's goatskin, he was safe from the dragon's venom.

To get the shield-rim free from the dragon's teeth, he had to tug at it so hard that his belt burst with the strain. To get the head of the spear from the dragon's heart, he had to tug at that so hard that his belt burst again.

At dawn, King Herrad went out to greet the sun. He came into his hall, and sat down on his high seat. Then Orm put on the goatskin hood and mask and longshirt and trousers, and went into the hall to the king.

Orm cast the iron spearhead and the golden scrap of shield-rim at King Herrad's feet. "Lord," he said, "it was I who slew the dragon. I come to claim my bride."

Tora Hart, too, was up with the sun. She cried to her servant girls, "Arise! We have slept too long. Today will be my wedding feast. Today's the day that my hero's longship will sail back to me."

They were happy as they put on arm rings and necklaces. Then King Herrad sent for them to go to him in his hall. As they went in, they saw Orm dressed in Ragnar's goatskins. They saw the spearhead and the shield-rim at King Herrad's feet.

"Your hero is soon here to claim you, princess," cried the servant girls.

"Is this he who slew the dragon?" asked King Herrad.

"Lord, it is," cried all the servant girls.

"Let me see his face," said Tora Hart.

Orm took the goatskin mask from his face. "This is not the one," said Tora Hart. "This is a servant."

"But so was the one who slew the dragon," cried the servant girls. "Do you not remember that we said so at the time?"

"Let me see his hair," said Tora Hart.

Orm put off his hood. Tora Hart saw that his hair was black and cut short.

"This is not the one," she said again. "This servant's hair is short and sooty. But the hair of the hero were long and as red as the sun."

"When did you see his hair, daughter?" asked King Herrad.

"When he stood at my tower gate," cried Tora Hart.

"We saw no red hair, princess," cried the servant girls.

"Are the goatskin trousers not the same?" asked King Herrad.

"They are," said Tora Hart. "But how did he get them?"

"I made them," said Orm.

"Is this not the spearhead," asked King Herrad, "that you told me had been left in the dragon's heart?"

"It is," said Tora Hart. "But does he have the shaft?"

"I had, but I burnt it," said Orm. "Its wood was full of venom."

"Is this not the gold the dragon bit from the shield-rim?" asked King Herrad.

"It is," said Tora Hart. "But does he have the shield?"

"I threw it into the sea," said Orm. "That, too, was full of venom."

"Sing me again the song you sang me then," said Tora Hart.

"It slips my mind," said Orm.

"Father," cried Tora Hart, "I swear this is not the hero who slew the dragon. My heart isn't warm to him as it was to the man who first wore the goatskin trousers."

"I was that man," said Orm. "It was I who slew the dragon. Lord, you swore that he who did so would win the princess as his bride."

"That vow must be kept, daughter," said King Herrad. "Be your hero servant or king, the wedding feast must be held today."

"Father," cried Tora Hart, "great evil will come on us if we hold the feast too quickly. Get the feast ready, if you must; but don't let me be married till the sun has set. If my hero has not come then, I will marry whichever man you want."

"So be it," said King Herrad.

8. Tora Hart's Wedding Feast

Tora Hart went from the hall to seek Kalf the Wiseman. She wept as she told him what had happened.

"Take heart, princess," said Kalf. "Put on your bridal dress, and take your place at the feast. Everything will be alright. Your hero will come."

So Tora Hart put on her bridal robe, and took her place at the feast. She did not look at Orm, at King Herrad's right hand. Time went on, and as it drew near to sunset, her hero had still not come.

Then her heart leapt for joy. For the lookout on the roof-ridge blew a note on his horn. It was the note that said a stranger was coming.

All wine cups were set down on the long table. All eyes were on the door.

In at that door came King Ragnar. Like a sun god he came in, his head bare, his long red hair held by a golden headband. His gold shoes were set with gems. Golden gloves were on his hands. His tunic was of fine cloth, dyed scarlet by the men of Gaul.

He came and stood in front of King Herrad. In his right hand was his spear shaft with no head. On his left arm was his round shield, with a gap in its golden rim.

He saw how Tora Hart sat on the high seat like a swan on a still wave, as white as the white swan beside her. And Tora Hart saw what goodness there was in him, and it made her own heart glad.

The spearhead and the golden scrap of shield-rim lay on the table before King Herrad. King Ragnar picked up the spearhead, to fit it to his spear shaft. He picked up the scrap of gold, to fit it to his shield-rim. Each slid into place.

"It seems this spear shaft has risen from the fire," said King Herrad. "And it seems this shield has risen from the sea."

Kalf the Wiseman rose from his seat. "Lord," he said to King Herrad, "this is King Ragnar of Denmark."

"I have won a nickname since we met, Lord Kalf," said King Ragnar. "It is King Goatskin."

Kalf went on, "It was to him I took my magic mirror with its image of the princess. He swore then to come and slay the dragon."

"And so he did!" cried Tora Hart.

"And to win the princess as his bride," said Kalf.

"And so he shall!" cried King Herrad.

He swung round in rage to Orm. But Orm was not there. From that day, he was never seen again in King Herrad's hall.

Then King Herrad rose, and led King Ragnar to Tora Hart. She said to him, "King Goatskin, my heart knows it was you who slew the dragon. But my servant girls seem to need more proof. Sing again the song you sang at my tower gate."

Then King Ragnar sang the song again:

Tora Hart-in-the-Tower,
Swan white, sun bright,
The dragon guards you now
Within your wall of gold.
Tora Hart-in-the-Tower,
Soon, soon you shall be free!

Then the servant girls all cried, "Now we know it was this king who slew the dragon!"

King Ragnar took the hand of Tora Hart in his. "Tora Hart, will you marry me?" he asked. And she told him, "King Goatskin, yes, and a thousand times yes."

Then Tora Hart and King Goatskin sat on the bridal bench. King Herrad made the wedding cross over them with his Thor hammer, and they were given the wedding mead to drink.

King Goatskin's men were sent for from his ship, to take part in the wedding feast. It kept going for a whole month; and each day the feast was more merry than the day before. From the best of golden wine cups they drank the best wine and mead.

At last, the wedding feast came to an end. The time came for King Goatskin to take his bride home. King Herrad said to him, "Take the dragon's gold, too, for that is Tora Hart's wedding gift."

King Goatskin said, "The love of Tora Hart is better to me than gold." But King Herrad told his men to bear the chests of gold down to the ship. And they did so.

Then King Goatskin led his bride by the hand, down the cliff path, and over the beach to the edge of the sea. Her white swan flew with her, just over her head. King Goatskin lifted Tora Hart in his arms, and placed her on his ship. Her white swan came to rest at her side.

All King Herrad's people stood on the beach to see them set sail, to wave and to call, "Fare you well, fare you well, Tora Hart!"

Queen Hild cried to her, "May your ship bring you home over calm seas, child, and your life, also."

King Herrad cried to her, "Live happy, my daughter!"

And the ship set sail.

9. TORA HART'S DEATHBED WISH

King Ragnar's ship carried Tora Hart to her new home over calm seas, her white swan at her side. When they landed in King Ragnar's harbour, a band of servant girls came to meet them in golden wagons. And Tora Hart rode with them to King Ragnar's hall, which stood a little way inland from the shore.

And here at Ledra, King Ragnar and Tora Hart lived happily. All the land grew to love the gentle queen and King Ragnar grew to be a great king. His fame went far and wide, and men said, "While Sigurd lived, Sigurd was the first and best of men. Now that Sigurd is dead, Ragnar takes his place."

When Tora Hart's first child was born, her servant girls carried it down from her room. They laid it at King Goatskin's feet as he sat on his high seat in his hall.

The king was glad when he saw it was a boy, big and strong. For Tora Hart was not strong, and he had been afraid that she might not give him strong sons. He called this first son Eric.

When Tora Hart's second child was born, it was another son. Again, the child was big and strong. King Goatskin called this second son Agnar.

But after fifteen years of happiness as Queen of Denmark, Tora Hart fell sick. King Goatskin hung the walls of her room with gilded animal skin, to keep her warm. On its floor he laid thick bearskins. But still she lay on her sickbed, and day by day she grew more frail.

Her white swan sat on the bed, by her hand. The queen said to it one day, "White swan, I think I won't live to be old."

"No," said the white swan. "Your death day is near, my queen."

"How can I help King Goatskin on that day?" asked Queen Tora Hart. "How can I heal his sadness?"

"My queen," said the white swan, "seven sons chose King Ragnar as father. Only two only have been born. Send him out to seek a mother for the other five."

"How will he find her?" Queen Tora Hart asked. And the white swan told her.

"I will do this," said Queen Tora Hart.

So when King Goatskin came up to her room, to sit by her bed, she said, "Goatskin, my much-loved Goatskin, when I die you must find a new queen."

"Never," said King Goatskin, "I will never marry again."

"Goatskin, my much-loved Goatskin," said Queen Tora Hart again, "you must go on a raid to find her. Take with you my golden headband, my silver belt and my scarlet shoes. The woman they fit is the woman you must marry."

"Never," said King Goatskin, "I will never marry again."

"Goatskin, my much-loved Goatskin," said Queen Tora Hart, "test her wit by this riddle. Tell her come to you not dressed, yet not undressed; alone, yet not alone; not fasting, yet not fed. If she can guess this riddle, she is the woman you must marry."

"Never," said King Goatskin, "I will never marry again."

"Goatskin, my much-loved Goatskin," said Queen Tora Hart, "take with you my dragon's gold. You got it as a wedding gift. Give it as a wedding gift when you find the woman you must marry."

"Never," said King Goatskin, "I will never marry again. Get well, my Tora Hart. You are the only wife I want."

But Queen Tora Hart did not get well. She died the next day at dawn.

King Goatskin told her servant girls to dress her in gold from head to foot. And he told his men to heap a great mound of stones and turf, to be her grave. And in this, on a bed of gold, they laid the dead queen.

From this mound her swan rose up on wide, snow-white wings. It sang a sad, sweet song. Then it flew away and it was never seen again in all the Northlands.

King Goatskin still said, "I will never marry again." But he had no peace because over and over, by day and by night, Queen Tora Hart's deathbed wish came back to him.

A year and a day passed. Then finally the King said to his men, "Bring out my longship from its winter shelter. We will sail forth on a raid." Gladly, the men ran to drag the longship out of its winter shelter, and down the beach to the edge of the sea.

Then King Goatskin said, "Take the chests of dragon gold, and put them in the ship's hold." The men did this, not so gladly.

Then King Goatskin took his dead queen's golden headband, and silver belt, and scarlet shoes, and went down to the harbour.

They slid the ship from its smooth rollers into the sea.

The blue and gold sails blew out. The oarsmen bent to the oars.

And so King Goatskin set sail, to seek his new queen.

10. The Child In The Harp

It was now sixteen years since Kalf the Wiseman had met the stranger in Mirkwood who had told him Sigurd the Dragon Slayer was dead. Kalf had then ridden the dark wood road that led to Denmark, while the stranger had ridden the dark wood road that led to Lymdale.

The stranger came at last to King Himir's hall in Lymdale. It was not like any other king's hall in all the Northlands, for it stood open to the green wood. It was made for the arts of peace rather than the darts of war.

While the stranger was still far off, harp music blew to him from that happy and open hall. When he rode up to the hall, the door stood wide open. He jumped down from his horse, and went in. King Himir, old and mild and good, stood by his high seat, playing the harp that was as tall as he was. On the high seat sat a child who was three years old. She wore a dress stiff with gold thread. Her golden hair hung soft as silk. Her skin was white, with rosy cheeks.

As the stranger came into the hall, her eyes met his. They were strange eyes, dark and bright, and as piercing as a hawk's. He felt his own drop before them, and said to himself, "This child must be Asla. Her gaze is too piercing for any man but Sigurd to be her father."

To King Himir he said, "Lord, I ride in haste, to tell

you that Sigurd is no more on this green earth. Hogni, his bloodbrother, killed him. And it is in Hogni's mind to seek Asla, Sigurd's child, and kill her too."

"Thank you, Sir Stranger," said old King Himir. "I will hide her well. She shall dress in rags, as if she were a servant's child. She shall stay with the other children and play with them till this danger is over."

"Lord," said the stranger, "no one will think she's a servant's child, with that hawk's gaze of hers. Can't you send her at once to another land? "

Asla spoke. "*You* can take me out of the land, foster-father," she said to the King. "You can hide me in your harp." For in the frame of King Himir's harp was a space big enough for a small child to creep into.

"That's a good plan, child," said the old King, "because then you can keep your golden dress, and I can dress in rags."

The stranger spent the night with King Himir and at dawn he rode away. King Himir put on rags, and left his hall. He put his harp on his back and in the frame of his harp was Asla.

From place to place he went, and from land to land. When they were out in the woods, far from anyone, Asla got out of the harp and ran and played in the sun. And when they came to a brook in the woods, she swam in it. With the music of his harp the King was able to draw down to earth the golden leeks that float unseen in the air, and with these he fed the child.

At dusk, he and Asla made huts of twigs to sleep in, out in the woods. This was a fine game to Asla because it was summer and still warm. But time went on, and summer drew to an end. Now it grew too cold for the child to sleep in the open air. Asla's hands and feet were so chilled in the night that she wept.

"Hush, pretty one," said King Himir. "We will try to find a roof to sleep under now that there is frost in the air."

At dusk next day they came out of the wood to a little farm that stood by the sea. Grass and wild flowers grew on its roof of turf, and a curl of smoke went up from the chimney.

"Oh, look, foster-father – a fire!" cried Asla. "Can we sleep here tonight?"

"Get into the harp, pretty one, and I will find out," said King Himir.

Asla crept into the harp, and he shut her in, and slung the harp on his back. He went past a herd of goats to the door of the little farm. As he knocked, it flew open.

An old woman stood there. She was dirty and ugly, with lank hair and a scowl on her face. Her name was Grima. King Himir asked her, "May I thaw my cold feet by your fire, good woman, then sleep in your grain loft?"

Her face grew yet more grim. She was just about to tell him to go away when she saw the glint of a golden arm ring amid his rags.

"Yes, stranger," she said. "Come and sit by the fire. And when you are warm, I will take you to the grain loft."

King Himir was glad to sit by the fire and to grow warm again. He set his harp down by his side, that Asla might feel the glow, too. The firelight fell on the harp; and as Grima sat down to spin, she saw a flash of gold in a crack in the harp frame. It was the hem of Asla's golden dress, that was not shut right in.

"Aha!" said Grima to herself. *"Gold on his arm; gold in his harp – this man is worth robbing."*

When King Himir was warm, he rose and picked up his harp, and Grima led him to the grain loft. Then she went back, and sat down to spin by the fire again. Soon her husband came in with the goats' milk.

"Aki," said Grima, "we have a guest in the grain loft. Go and kill him while he sleeps."

But Aki said, "Grima, it is a bad thing to kill a guest. And it is a bad thing to kill a man while he sleeps. So that is two bad things you ask me do."

"He has a golden arm ring on his arm," Grima told him, "and more gold in his harp."

"Killing him is not such a bad thing, then," said Aki.

He slid his dagger into his belt, and he crept out to the grain loft. With one stab in the dark, he killed the old King as he slept. Grima had crept out at his heels. Now she said, aloud, "Take the arm ring. It's on his right arm."

Her loud voice woke Asla as she lay in the warm straw. In the dark she shrank and shook with fear. Then she crept into the one safe place she knew. She crept into the harp, and pulled the door fast shut.

"Now help me to lift the harp," said Grima. Aki did so. "If this is all gold!" he said, "we'll be rich for life."

They took the harp from the grain loft, and set it down by the fire. "I can't see any gold now," said Grima. "That's odd. There must be a way into the frame." They tried to find it; but the door was shut too tight. "Then we must smash the frame to get at the gold," said Grima.

So Aki took a big stone, and broke the harp open with one blow. In the frame they found no gold, but they found Asla, in her golden dress.

11. ASLA TURNS INTO KRAKA

"Now, who can you be?" Grima asked the child in the harp. "Where do you come from? What is your name?"

Asla shut her lips tight, and made no sound. But her eyes were so piercing in the firelight that they made Aki drop his own gaze.

"Don't tell me to kill the child as well," said Aki, "for that I will not do."

"No, we will keep the child," said Grima. "She can help me with the farm tasks. We will say she is our own child."

"But what if she says she is not?" asked Aki.

"She is mute, so how can she?" said Grima.

"You only have to look at her," said Aki, "to see she is not our own child, with that golden hair, and her skin so white."

"She will not stay like that for long," said Grima. "I will make her look like our own child. I will cut off her golden hair, and dirty her face. I'll dress her in black rags, with a cap of tar on her head."

"What shall we call her?" asked Aki.

"We will call her Kraka, Little Crow," said Grima.

So Grima cut off Asla's golden hair, and dirtied her face. She took off her golden dress and dressed her in black rags. She put a cap of tar on her head and gave her a bed of straw to sleep on.

But Asla did not sleep that night. All night she lay and wept. She wept for good King Himir, her kind foster-father. She wept for the harp that had, for so long, been her safe home. She wept for the golden hair Grima had cut off her head, and for the golden dress Grima had torn off her back.

At dawn next day she crept from her straw and ran out into the green wood. She ran till she came to a pool and she bent to drink from it. In the pool she saw a little black crow of a child, dressed in black rags, with a cap of tar on her shorn head, and with dirty skin.

"Oh no! Oh no!" she cried angrily. "I will not stand it! I will run away!"

Three black-and-white magpies sat on the branch of a tree over the pool. "Did you hear that?" said one of the magpies. "She says she will run away. But why, when here she is safe, and Sigurd's enemies will never find her?"

"Even if they come here," said the next magpie, "they will never think that this little black crow is golden Asla. The dirt and the rags and the cap of tar will keep her safe from them."

"And if she runs away," said the third magpie, "she will not be here when the king who is to marry her comes for her."

Asla dried her eyes. "Thank you, kind magpies," she said, and she felt less sad as she ran back to the farm.

She was glad now to be at the farm, since it hid her from her father's enemies. She was glad of her black crow garb, since it kept her safe. She did not mind the hard tasks Grima gave her to do. She did not even mind when Grima beat her. For she knew now that she was not here forever. She knew now that a king was to marry her, and that she was here only till he came to find her.

But still she never spoke to Grima or to Aki, but only to the three magpies, and to Aki's dog, and to Grima's herd of goats.

Each day Grima sent her out into the green wood to tend the herd of goats. Each day, Aki's dog went with her. Each day he lay by her as she sat by the pool. Each day the three magpies sat on the branch of the tree and spoke with her.

"Wash off the old dirt each dawn in this pool, Kraka-Asla," the first magpie told her. "Smear on new dirt at dusk when you go back to Grima. We will show you the best dew to make your skin stay white under it."

"Your golden hair will soon grow again, Kraka-Asla," the next magpie told her. "Brush it each day by this pool. When it is long, we will show you how to bind it up under your cap of tar so that Grima will not see it."

"Do not eat the dry crusts Grima gives you, Kraka-Asla," the third magpie told her. "We will show you how to draw down golden leeks out of the air, the same as King Himir fed you with."

"Give Grima's food to Aki's dog, Kraka-Asla," the first magpie told her.

"Make a pet of him, Kraka-Asla," the second magpie told her.

"For the time will come when you will need a dog, Kraka-Asla," the third magpie told her.

"Bring hair from your goats, Kraka-Asla," said the first magpie.

"We will teach you how to make it into a net, Kraka-Asla," said the second magpie.

"For the time will come when you will need a net, Kraka-Asla," said the third magpie.

"Bring meal from the grain loft, Kraka-Asla," said the first magpie.

"We will teach you how to make bread, Kraka-Asla," said the second magpie.

"For the time will come when you will need to make bread, Kraka-Asla," said the third magpie.

Kraka-Asla did everything that the magpies told her.

So the days and the weeks and the months and the years went by, till it was sixteen years since she had left Lymdale in King Himir's harp. And all this time, as far as Grima and Aki knew, she was still mute.

She grew into a tall, strong woman. Under the dirt, her skin was still white. Under the cap of tar, her golden hair grew again till it was so long that it fell to the grass when she let it down.

Each day she came to the pool to wash and to brush her hair. Each day she spoke with the three wise magpies, and did everything that they told her. Each day she ate golden leeks that she drew down out of the air.

And each day her piercing eyes swept the sea for the ship of the king who was to come and marry her.

12. King Goatskin Finds Kraka

The day came when Kraka saw a longship skim over the sea. She saw the flash of shields along its sides. She saw it sail into the harbour under the little farm. She saw a band of its shipmen spring to land and stride up the beach.

One of them carried a big sack that looked like a bag of grain.

Kraka left her herd of goats and went to meet them, Aki's dog at her side. She was fresh from the pool; her skin was free from dirt and was smooth and white with rosy cheeks. She had taken off her cap of tar to brush her hair; it fell to her feet over her black rags in a cloak of gold, as soft as silk.

The men stood still when they saw her, eyes round at the sight of such a woman on this wild beach.

"What are you doing here?" she asked.

The one with the bag of grain told her, "We saw your roof from our ship, good woman, and our king sent us with grain, to make into bread."

Kraka's heart began to beat fast. "Your king? Who is your king?" she asked him.

And he told her, "King Ragnar Goatskin, King of Denmark."

Kraka led them in. She went past Grima as if she did not see her.

"Give me the grain," said Kraka. "I will make your king his bread."

Grima gasped as the long cloak of golden hair swung apart to show the black rags under it. "Can this be Kraka?" she cried. "But can Kraka speak? Does Kraka have golden hair? Who told Kraka how to make bread? Give me the grain, Kraka. If the bread is for a king, I should make it."

But Kraka's gaze was so piercing that it made Grima look away.

"Leave the woman alone, old crone," said the men. "The bread will be all the better for being made by such fair hands."

Kraka made the bread with deft hands. Loaf by loaf she gave it to the shipmen. "Put them in the oven to bake," she told them, "and take care not to let them burn." But Kraka was so pretty that the men forgot all about the bread, and let it burn.

They filled the sack with burnt bread and carried it down the beach to the ship. But one of the shipmen ran back and took out his knife; he cut off a strand of Kraka's long golden hair, and laid it in a fold of white cloth. Then he, too, ran down to the ship.

King Goatskin cut a loaf and sat down to eat. "This bread is well-made," he said. "I've never eaten better. Who made it?"

"Kraka, the peasant's daughter, lord," the shipmen told him.

"How did you let such good bread burn?" King Goatskin asked.

"We had better things than bread to look at, lord," they told him.

"What can be better than bread?" King Goatskin asked.

"Kraka, the peasant's daughter," said the men.

"Why, what was she like?" asked the King.

And the men told him, "Her skin is white with rosy cheeks, lord, and her hair is long and golden. We haven't seen a woman as fair since Queen Tora Hart died."

"A peasant's daughter, as fair as my queen?" cried King Goatskin. "Men, are you out of your wits?" But then the man who had cut off the lock of Kraka's hair took it from the fold of white cloth. He set it in King Goatskin' hands.

King Goatskin was still for a long time. At last he said, "Yes, it is as long and as golden as my Tora Hart's. I must see this woman with my own eyes. Tell her to come to me here on my longship, not dressed, yet not undressed, alone yet not alone, not fasting yet not fed."

One of the men left the ship and went up the beach. Kraka came to the door with Grima at her heels. "King Goatskin asks for you to come to him on his longship," he told Kraka. "He asks that you come not dressed yet not undressed, alone yet not alone, not fasting yet not fed. "

"And if I come like this?" asked Kraka.

"Then I think he will marry you," he told her.

"Tell him I will come," she said.

"Kraka!" cried Grima. "You shall not go!" But the shipman said, "be quiet, old crone. This is the King's will." And the look Kraka gave her was so piercing that she shrank back and said no more.

Then Kraka went into the grain loft. She put off her black rags and bound the net of goat hair around her. Over it fell the long cloak of her golden hair. So she was not dressed and yet not undressed.

"Come!" she cried to Aki's dog. And she ran down the

beach to the longship with the dog at her side. So she went alone and yet not alone.

As she came to the ship, she drew down a golden leek out of the air. She bit it, then let it float away. So she came not fasting and yet not fed.

She stood in front of King Goatskin, and he saw that she was as fair as his men had told him. He held out to her Queen Tora Hart's golden headband. She bound it around her brow. It was as if it was made for her.

He held out to her Queen Tora Hart's silver belt. She put it around her hips. It was as if it was made for her.

He held out to her Queen Tora Hart's scarlet shoes. She slid her white feet into them. It was as if they were made for her.

He asked her then, "Will you come with me, Kraka the Peasant's Daughter, and be my queen?" And she told him: "King Goatskin, yes, and a thousand times yes."

"That's what Tora Hart said at our wedding feast," said King Goatskin, and he felt a pang in his heart.

A loud shout came from the beach, and they saw Aki stride down to the edge of the sea. His dog sprang from the ship, and ran to meet him. "King," Aki cried, "my wife tells me it is your will to marry our daughter. How will we manage when we are old? We rely on her."

King Goatskin said to him, "You shall have gold to keep you comfortable for the rest of your life." And to his men he said, "Set the chests of dragon's gold on the beach. For the love of Kraka the Peasant's Daughter is better to me than gold."

The men did so, but not gladly. "He said the same about Tora Hart," said one man to the next. "That time we took the gold, now we're throwing it away," said the other.

Three magpies flew from the green wood and over the beach to the longship. They came to rest on the mast.

"You will still need us, Queen Kraka," said the first.

"You will need us more than ever now you are a queen, Queen Kraka," said the second.

"So we shall sail with you, Queen Kraka," said the third, "and live near you."

The shipmen slid the longship off the beach into the sea, then swung over the sides and sat down, each at his oar.

"Live happy, my daughter!" Aki cried from the beach.

"That's what King Herrad shouted to Tora Hart," said one Dane to the next.

"Then a king's daughter; now a peasant's daughter," said the first. "I don't think this bridal will be as good."

And the ship set sail.

13. Sibilya Plots To Marry King Goatskin

King Ragnar's ship carried Kraka the Peasant's Daughter to her new home over calm seas, her three black-and-white magpies on its mast. When they came to land in King Ragnar's harbour, a band of servant girls came to meet them in golden wagons. And Kraka the Peasant's Daughter rode with them to King Ragnar's hall.

Here, for a month, they had the wedding feast. After her hard life with Grima, it was like a rich dream to Kraka – tables spread with silk, wine in cups of gold, robes and gems like she hadn't seen since she was a child in Lymdale.

A bond of love soon grew between Queen Kraka and her stepsons, Eric and Agnar. But many people didn't like having a peasant's daughter as queen. Nor did they like those eyes like a hawk's, that made their own drop before them. Nor did they forget the dragon's gold that had been left as bridal price with Aki.

When Queen Kraka's first son was born, he had no bones. "See what comes of a peasant's daughter queen!" said those who did not love her. "Will King Goatskin let a child with no bones live?"

But when the child was laid at his feet, King Goatskin let him live. "What he lacks in bones he will make up for in wit," he said.

And he called him Ivar. So from the day of his birth men gave the boy the nickname of Ivar Lackbones.

Queen Kraka's next son was as strong as Ivar Lackbones was weak. He was so strong that the day he was born, he burst the linen bands that he had been wrapped in.

King Goatskin called him Born. But from the day of his birth men gave him the nickname of Born Ironsides.

Queen Kraka's next two sons were twins. They were strong, but not so strong as Born Ironsides. King Goatskin called them White-Sark and Rogvold.

Each spring, when the corn had been sown, King Goatskin went on raids far and wide. He won battle after battle, till he had won more battles than he had lived years. He was known all over the Northlands as the first and best of men.

As Queen Tora Hart's sons, Eric and Agnar, grew tall, King Goatskin took them with him on his raids. Then, day by day, their four small stepbrothers kept watch on the sea for their homecoming. Loud were the shouts of joy they gave when they saw the dragon prows of the longships. Night after night, they sat with wide eyes and drank in the tales Eric and Agnar told them of far lands they had seen.

By day, Eric and Agnar took them out to the field for trials of skill, to train them in all the arts of war. Even Ivar Lackbones was not left out, for the two big stepbrothers set him on a shield, and carried him with them. From his shield, Ivar was able to throw a spear and draw a bow as well as any of his brothers.

And he had other skills that they did not have. He often

sat alone on his shield outside Queen Kraka's window. And her magpies flew to him here, to teach him skill in magical verses, and how to plan a battle, to have foresight, to have farsight, and to make up in wit for his lack of bones.

So, in spite of those who did not love a peasant's daughter queen, all went well in King Goatskin's hall, and Queen Kraka's sons began to grow tall.

Now the King of Sweden at that time was King Egill. He was the lord of wide lands and many men, and in his day he had been a man of might. But now he grew sick in his old age and he had no son to lead his army for him.

He did have a daughter, Sibilya, who had dark hair. So he said to her, "Daughter, I grow tired and I'm too old to guard my land. Choose a husband, a man of fame; I will make him lord of all my army, and he shall be king in my place when I die."

Princess Sibilya told him, "I will marry only King Ragnar of Denmark, for he is the first and best of men."

"But he has a queen, daughter," said the old King.

"She is low-born, a peasant's daughter," said Sibilya. "A king is free to send such a wife away from him."

"But will he wish to?" asked King Egill. "Even to marry you?"

'With all you have to offer him as a wedding gift," said the dark princess, "I do not think it will be hard to part them."

King Egill thought hard, his hand in his long white beard. "It is good advice, daughter," he said at last. "I shall have strong help in him. No king will be as great as I if I have him to lean on. I may never get such a son-in-law again. And with him I shall have grandsons of great fame."

"Be wary, Father," said Sibilya. "Do not let him see your plans too soon."

So King Egill sent one of his lords to seek out King Goatskin in his hall at Ledra. "Lord," he said, "King Egill of Sweden sends me to remind you of the love he bears you. He begs you to visit him, that you and your men may be given helmets and shields, swords and coats of mail, cups and arm rings of gold."

At this, the bright hall seemed to go dark to Queen Kraka, but she didn't know why. She cried swiftly to King Goatskin, "Is our own treasure house not already full of such things?"

But King Goatskin's Viking men cried back as swiftly, "Not as full as it was before the king paid Tora Hart's dragon's gold as a bridal price for Kraka the Peasant's Daughter."

"Ragnar," said Queen Kraka, "I feel it in my bones that it will be a bad thing for you to go." But again the Vikings cried out, "It will be a bad thing not to go, when King Egill holds out gold with both hands."

King Goatskin held up his hand to quieten the noise. "Tell King Egill, I will visit him," he told the Swedish lord.

14. Sibilya Brews A Love Potion For King Goatskin

So King Goatskin got ready to visit King Egill. "Why don't you want me to go?" he asked Queen Kraka.

"I do not trust that old king," she told him. "I think he plans more than meets the eye."

"What more can he plan?" asked King Goatskin. "In any case, I've given my word to go, and I must stand by it."

"Be wary in Sweden, my Goatskin," said Queen Kraka. "Drink as little as you can, because wine can steal away wit."

"All will be well – you will see, my Kraka," said King Goatskin. And he set sail with his Vikings for King Egill's hall at Uppsala.

There was a warm welcome in that hall. The two kings sat on the high seat, and drank the best wine happily. At the feast that night, Princess Sibilya came into the hall, to bring a special cup to the guest. As she gave him the cup, she spoke sweetly to him, but he was hardly aware of her, for her hair was as black as a raven, and both the queens he had loved had been golden. And he still loved Queen Kraka.

When King Egill was alone with Sibilya, he asked her, "Well, daughter, what do you think of King Goatskin, now you have seen him again?"

"Father, my heart has not smiled on any man as much as him. But his heart doesn't smiles on me. His heart smiles only on his low-born queen. It seems I must brew him a love potion, to turn his love from her."

Sibilya was, in fact, a witch. So she took a wine cup, and on it she cut spells. Into the wine she put dark herbs and other bad things. She sang strong spells over it. At that night's feast, she went into the hall again and gave the love potion to King Goatskin to drink.

He drank, and as he gave the cup back to her, his eyes noticed on her for the first time. He thought she the most beautiful thing he'd seen, and his heart grew warm for her.

"Ah, princess," he cried, "if only I wasn't married!"

"What then?" she asked, with a slow, sly smile.

"Ah, then," said he, "I would choose you for my queen above all others under the sun."

"Your wife is a peasant's daughter," she said. "A low-born queen can be sent away."

"She has given me four sons," he told her. "And if Tora Hart saw her clearly as she lay on her deathbed, she will give me a fifth yet."

But Sibilya made herself soft and kind to him, in her ways and in her words. She spoke with his Vikings, and was glad when she found they had no love for Queen Kraka. She encouraged them to nag King Goatskin to get rid of his low-born wife.

Gradually, by her cunning, she drew the heart of King Goatskin away from Queen Kraka, till at last he asked her, "Sibilya, how soon will you marry me?"

"As soon as you are free," she told him. "Go back to Ledra, and send away your low-born wife. We will hold the wedding feast as soon as you return, and my father will make you lord of all his army." So King Goatskin and his Vikings set sail at once for Denmark.

Queen Kraka's heart was heavy when she woke that dawn. She rose and went out, and sat down on the bench outside her window. Her three magpies flew to her.

She asked them, "What news is there of Goatskin?"

"He is on his way home," said the first.

"But not to stay," said the second.

"Only to put you away," said the third.

"Then he will go back," said the first.

"And marry King Egill's daughter," said the second.

"And be lord of all his army," said the third.

Queen Kraka felt her heart stop. "Is this his own free wish?" she asked.

"No," said the first. "The princess caused it."

"She gave him a love potion to drink," said the second, "to turn his heart from you."

"Not till he had drunk it," said the third, "did her plan work."

Queen Kraka sat as still and as white as someone who had died. At last she rose, went into her room, and shut the door.

Her sons and her stepsons came to her room, to ask if she was sick. The others carried Ivar Lackbones up the stone stair on his shield.

Queen Kraka sent one of her servant girls out to tell them, "She is not sick, but she will not see you, for her heart is heavy."

"Go in to her," said Ivar Lackbones as he sat on his shield. "Ask her why she sits alone with heavy heart. Tell her that her sadness is our sadness."

The servant went in to the queen. She came out again to tell them, "She sends you word that you will know everything as soon as the king arrives."

The others carried Ivar Lackbones down from the queen's room on his shield. They set him down in the porch of the hall.

His eyes, as piercing as his mother's, were on the sea. "I see our father's ship," he said. "We shall not have to wait long."

15. KRAKA TURNS BACK INTO ASLA

King Goatskin came up from the harbour to his hall. Queen Kraka did not run from the hall to meet him, as she normally did. But Ivar Lackbones sat in the doorway on his shield, and his three brothers and his two stepbrothers stood behind him. Each face was stern.

"Father," said Ivar Lackbones, "what is this sadness you've brought upon our mother?"

King Goatskin was surprised, but he told his sons the truth. "I'm thinking of sending her away. But how did she know this?"

"Why do you want to send her away?" Ivar Lackbones asked.

"She is too low-born to be my queen," said King Goatskin.

"Her low birth is no new thing," said Ivar Lackbones. "Yet you have lived with her happily all these years. And she has lived her life loved by us all, both sons and stepsons. Why then, all at once, do you want to send her away?"

"So that I can marry a new wife, " said King Goatskin.

At this, all six brothers gave a growl of rage. "You gave our mother your word," White-Sark cried. "And you should keep to your word."

"You will regret this deed if you do it," Rogvold cried. "If you do this deed, it will throw us into conflict, for all four of her sons will stand by her."

"Her two stepsons, also," said Eric. "For in all things, she has been like a mother to us."

"Yes, never in this house," said Agnar, "did stepbrother fight brother. For she gave peace and love to all of us alike."

It was Born Ironsides who asked, "Who is the new wife that you want to marry?"

And King Goatskin told them, "Sibilya, the Princess of Sweden."

"You must know full well that she won you through cunning and deceit," said Ivar Lackbones. "Did she brew you a love potion? And did our mother not warn you that wine can steal away wit?"

Then Queen Kraka spoke from within the hall. "It was a bad day when your father went to Sweden. It was a bad woman he met. It will be bad things that she brings him."

The brothers swung round. Queen Kraka stood with her back to a pillar, her arms flat on its wood.

"Kraka," said King Goatskin, "I am glad I need not tell my news again. For my sons tell me you know that I am here to send you away. Go back, I beg you, to the land I took you from."

Kraka stood still. Then she said, "I would be very sad to be widow. But this makes me sadder still, that you send me away, the love between us dead."

"It is not out of lack of love I send you away," King Goatskin told her. "For now that I see you again, I know that Sibilya won me for a time with deceit, but that I still love you, yes, even better than I knew."

"Then why?" cried Queen Kraka. "Then why?"

And King Goatskin told her, "I have come to see that it is not good for a land when a king marries a low-born queen. I have come to see the conflict it breeds among his men."

"Is that all?" cried Queen Kraka. "Look in my eyes, then, Goatskin!"

King Goatskin tried to hold her eyes with his, but he had to drop his own before her piercing gaze.

"Is that the gaze of a peasant's daughter?" she asked. "Or of the daughter of a king?"

King Goatskin gave a shout of joy, "Of a king! But what king?"

"I am not Kraka the Peasant's Daughter, " she said. "I am Asla, Sigurd's Daughter."

And she told him of her life with King Himir in Lymdale, and of all that happened to her after Sigurd was killed.

"Take heart, king's daughter," said King Goatskin then. "No other king's daughter shall send you away from me."

"Soon, I will have another son," Queen Asla told him. "And as proof that he is Sigurd's grandson, he will have a dragon in his right eye."

"I need no proof but your own eyes," cried King Goatskin. "Asla is better to me than anything else; I will lay down my life rather than lose her love."

So again their hearts drew close to each other, and they were happy.

Then King Goatskin had the news told to all the Danes that the name of their queen was not Kraka, but Asla, and that she was no peasant's daughter, but the child of Sigurd the Dragon Slayer. And all were glad to think that they had as queen the child of such a famous hero. The Vikings felt ashamed for the mean things they had said about her, and they all swore to be true to her.

Soon after this, Queen Asla's fifth son was born and laid at the feet of the king.

When King Goatskin saw how big and strong the boy was he was glad, and glad when he saw the piercing eyes of the child, and still more glad when he saw the dragon shape in the child's right iris.

He called him Sigurd. And from the day of his birth, men gave him the nickname of Sigurd Snake-in-the-Eye.

So now all was peace and joy in King Goatskin's hall. But Queen Asla's heart was still heavy as she thought, "There are bad things still to come from that journey to Sweden. I do not think Sibilya will hear this news with joy!"

16. SIBILYA WANTS WAR

A Dane rode up to King Egill's hall at Uppsala.

"What is the news from Denmark?" the old king asked with a smile. "How soon will my son-in-law be here to hold the wedding feast?"

"Not soon, lord," the Dane told him. "For his queen is no longer Kraka the Peasant's Daughter, but Asla, Sigurd's Daughter. So he is no longer going to send her away."

At this news Sibilya shrieked loudly. "Daughter," said King Egill, "that is not a happy sound."

Sibilya sprang to her feet and ran out of the hall and up to her room. She sat down and picked up her needle. But soon she threw down the scarlet silk, ripping it in two. Then her rage broke out, and the sound and the fury of it rang far and wide round the hall. Up she sprang, stamping to and fro, and at last she ran into the wildwood, to shriek her rage amid the howls of the wolves.

When she came back to her father's hall, her face was grim. She said to him, "Out of this shall come his death, or her death, or your death, or my death."

"We can attack him with our warriors," said King Egill. "But who will lead them? I'm too old."

"Tell them to get ready to fight," said Sibilya, her lips thin. "They will be led."

The Dane went back in haste to King Goatskin's hall at Ledra. "Lord," he cried, "the Swedish warriors are getting ready to attack you!"

"Who is leading them? asked King Goatskin. "Not King Egill, for he is sick and old."

"Lord, no one knows," he was told. "But the Princess Sibilya has sworn that they will be led."

Queen Asla went out, and sat on the bench outside her window. Her three magpies flew to her. She asked them, "Is this war King Egill's or Sibilya's?"

"Sibilya's," said the first magpie. "She can't sleep for the bitterness in her heart for King Goatskin."

"She doesn't forget her sadness, but broods over it," said the second.

"She longs to bring shame upon the king," said the third.

"Her pride and her rage will be hard to overcome," said the first.

"Many men will pay with their lives," said the second.

"She has sworn that it shall end in King Goatskin's death, or King Egill's death, or her death, or your death," said the third.

"But it will not be King Egill's," said the first.

"Nor will it be yours," said the second.

"It lies between King Goatskin's and her own," said the third.

"Then it should be hers," said Queen Asla, "for she is the source of all this sadness."

"Then you must keep King Goatskin back from this war," said the magpies.

"I will do that," said Queen Asla. And she rose, and went in, and spoke to her stepsons about it.

Agnar and Eric were glad to help. They came to King

Goatskin, and said, "Father, King Egill is too old to lead his army. So it will be better if you do not lead ours. Send us two to lead them in your place."

King Goatskin thought deeply, then said, "Go then, my sons."

So word was sent round the land to call in the warriors, and the shipmen got the fleet ready. Queen Asla took Eric aside and she gave him a ring. "May all go well for you, fair foster-son," she said. "But if it goes badly, send back this ring to me."

King Goatskin and Queen Asla went down to the harbour with their five sons, to see Eric and Agnar set out to sea. "Fare you well, my sons," said Queen Asla to her stepsons. "And may you come back safe to me."

And Eric and Agnar told her, "Let it go as it will, Mother, as long as you remain happy."

Then, with their warriors, they set sail for Sweden.

17. The Witch Cow Wins The Battle

When the Danes came to the field of battle, they gasped. For the Swedish warriors were not led by a man. They were led by a huge white cow.

It was soon clear that that cow was a witch cow, for in that battle she killed more Danes than all the Swedes. She only had to gore a man with her horns, or kick a man, or even look at a man, and that man died.

The first Dane she killed was Agnar. When Eric saw this, he drew one of his men aside and gave him Queen Asla's ring. "I smell witchcraft here," he said. "If I am right, that witch cow will soon seek me out, and kill me as she killed my brother. If I die, take this ring to Queen Asla, and tell her that she has a witch cow as her enemy."

The man saw the witch cow seek Eric out, just as he had said. He saw her gore him, he saw him fall. He went to him; he found him dead.

Many a sword struck that witch cow. Many a spear was thrown at her. Many an arrow flew at her. But it was as if a charm kept her safe. The power of the witch cow was too mighty for the Danes. With the witch cow's help, it was not hard in the end for the Swedes to win that battle.

Then Eric's man set sail for Ledra in haste. He came quickly to King Goatskin's hall, and gave him news of his lost sons and their lost battle. He gave Queen Asla her ring. "Prince Eric's last words," he told her, "were that you had a witch cow as your enemy."

Queen Asla went out to her five sons. They were under the porch of the hall. Four of them stood, fitting shafts to their bows. Ivar Lackbones sat on his shield, and cut special verses in the shaft of his spear. Queen Asla cried out to them, "Never again will you see your two brothers in this hall. Never again will you see them sing or play the harp, play chess, or any other game."

"Mother," said Ivar Lackbones, "we were all seven sons of one father. You don't need to tell us what to do; we already want to do it. Tell us how our brothers died."

Queen Asla told them. "Eric's last words were," she said, "that I have a witch cow as my enemy."

"Born," said Ivar Lackbones, "take me to outside our mother's window." Born Ironsides lifted him up, and set him down on the bench under Queen Asla's window. Her three magpies flew to him.

"What can kill a witch cow?" he asked them.

"Only a bold horse," said the first magpie.

"It must have wheels," said the second.

"And fire inside it," said the third.

"Show me how to make one," said Ivar Lackbones.

"We will," said all three.

So, with their help, he made a brazen horse. He gave it wheels and made a place for a fire inside it. Then the five brothers went to King Goatskin. "Father, this is now our war," they said. "Our brothers were killed. So give us permission to send out word round the land again, and to set sail with fresh ships."

"I will go, and you shall go with me," said King Goatskin.

But Queen Asla cried out to him, "No, Goatskin, no! You have won your fame and glory. Let your sons win glory, too."

So again, word was sent round the land, to call up new warriors. The shipmen got a new fleet ready. Born Ironsides carried Ivar Lackbones on his shield to the prow of the first longship. Born and White-Sark and Rogvold and little Sigurd Snake-in-the-Eye stood around the shield.

King Goatskin and Queen Asla went down to the harbour, to see their five sons set out to sea. "Fare you well, my sons," said Queen Asla. "And may you come back safe to me."

And her five sons told her, "Let it go as it will, Mother, as long as you remain happy."

Then, with their warriors, and with Ivar Lackbones' brazen horse, they set sail for Sweden.

18. Ivar Lackbones Slays The Witch Cow

The Danish longships came to rest in a Swedish harbour, and the five brothers led the warriors on to land and got them ready for battle, rank on rank.

They didn't have long to wait before they met the Swedish warriors. Men fell thick; the field was red with blood. And again it was the white witch cow that led the Swedes; again she had but to gore a man with her horns, or kick a man, or even look at a man, and that man died.

White-Sark and Rogvold, Born Ironsides and little Sigurd Snake-in-the-Eye led the Danes. They shouted aloud to fight with all their might. But Ivar Lackbones lit a fire in his brazen horse at the rear of the Danish warriors, and had himself lifted on to its back.

Then he let out a great war shout, and the Danes made a lane for him to the front of their army. And along that lane sped the brazen horse on its wheels, with Ivar Lackbones on its back, his shield set up before him.

The brazen horse sped right at the witch cow, in a cloud of black smoke. She fell, and the heavy wheels went over her. She did not rise, and when men ran to her, they found not a white cow, but the dead form of a dark maiden.

When they lifted her up, they saw it was Princess Sibilya.

The news flew among both warriors that the witch cow had been killed. From then on, the power of the Danes was too mighty for the Swedes. It was not hard in the end for the Danes to win that battle.

Rogvold died in that fight. When it came to an end, the four brothers who were left cast lots as to who was to be king of Sweden, and Born Ironsides was chosen. So White-Sark and Ivar Lackbones and Sigurd Snake-in-the Eye left him in King Egill's hall at Upsala, with part of the Danish army; and with the rest they set sail for home with the good news.

And when Queen Asla saw the longships out at sea, she threw off her cloak and ran down to the harbour to meet her sons, to clasp them in her arms, and to bring them in with all love. They told her how Sibilya had taken the shape of the witch cow, and how Ivar Lackbones, with his brazen horse, had killed her in that shape.

"She did a bad thing to herself with her witchcraft and her shape-shifting," they said. "It brought her to her death. Yet not before she had caused the death of many good Danes."

After this first taste of battle, the three Danish princes found it hard to stay at home. "Give us a longship each," they said to King Goatskin, "and permission to sail on a raid, that we may travel out into the wide world and get fame and gold."

So King Goatskin gave them longships. They went raiding far and wide, and had many battles, and won them all, Ivar Lackbones on his brazen horse between his brothers. In this way they won the land of the Wends, and cast lots as to who was to be its king. And White-Sark was chosen.

When the winter gales arrived, Ivar Lackbones and Sigurd Snake-in-the-Eye went home to Ledra, with many ships and much gold. Then huge fires were lit along King Goatskin's hall, and when his men sat by them at night, his two sons told of the far lands they had been in, and of the strange sights they had seen.

19. Ragnar Goatskin Sails To England

As soon as the spring corn was sown, the two princes got ready for a new raid. The longships came out of their winter shelter, and the great waves carried them far away.

Then King Goatskin began to long to go raiding, too. He said to Queen Asla, "It is time I did deeds as great as those of our sons."

Queen Asla felt her blood run cold with foresight of bad things to come. "You have done them already," she said. "Your name is the most famous in all the Northlands."

"Then I must stop that fame getting rusty," said King Goatskin.

"At least wait till our sons come back," said Queen Asla, "and let them go with you."

"It is best for them to win their fame alone," King Goatskin said.

"What land are you thinking of troubling?" asked Queen Asla, with a sigh.

"England," he told her.

Queen Asla rose, and went out, and sat down on the bench outside her window. Her three magpies flew to her.

"Should the king go raiding to England?" she asked them.

"If he goes to England," said the first, "you will wake to great sadness."

"Evil came from his travels to Sweden," said the second. "But more evil still will come if he sails to England."

"From Sweden he came back to you," said the third. "He will not come back from England."

Queen Asla rose and went back to the hall with a heavy heart. She sat down on the high seat by the side of King Goatskin. She laid her hand on his. "Goatskin, you will regret this deed if you do it," she said. "You will go to your own doom. Trouble some other land, if you must; but do not go to England."

"My mind is made up," said King Goatskin.

"You will be short of longships," said Queen Asla, "till our sons come back."

"I have three great merchant ships," King Goatskin told her. "Each will hold five hundred men. I will take those."

"It will not be wise to sail to England in such big ships," said Queen Asla. "The tides and sandbanks on that coast will trap them."

"My mind is made up," said King Goatskin.

"It will be stormy till next new moon," said Queen Asla. "At least wait till this moon is over."

"My mind is made up," said King Goatskin. "I will sail at once."

"Wait at least while I finish a magic shirt," said Queen Asla, "for you to wear to keep you safe from harm in England."

While King Goatskin got his three big merchant ships ready, Queen Asla sat in her room to finish the magic shirt. For its magic to have power, it had to be made in seven lands. Hun servants had grown the flax; Saxon servants had beaten the flax; Norse servants had spun the flax; Frankish servants had woven the flax; one arm was made by the Irish, the other by the Finns. And now Queen Asla made the rest of the shirt in Denmark.

And as she made it, she sang this song of power over it:

> *Seven toils,*
> *Seven soils,*
> *Are in this shirt.*
> *Songs I sing over it;*
> *Songs I stitch into it –*
> *Songs of power,*
> *And of holy magic.*
> *Dressed in this shirt,*
> *Flesh will not bleed;*
> *Spear will not strike;*
> *Sword will not bite;*
> *Snake will not sting;*
> *Flood will not drown.*
> *Dressed in this shirt,*
> *Ragnar the Dragon Slayer*
> *Stands far from his death hour!*

When the magic shirt was made, Queen Asla gave it to King Goatskin and he put it on. And her blood ran less cold when at the last she went down with him to his merchant ships in the harbour. She said to him, as she had said to Tora Hart's sons, and then to her own sons, "Fare you well, my Goatskin. And may you come back safe to me."

And he said to her, as his sons had said, "Let it go as it will, my Asla, as long as you remain happy."

At that she burst out, "How can I be happy when you're going to I know not what bad fate? Ah, how often must the wisdom of women give way to the might of men!"

This was their last parting, and they each went their way. King Goatskin set sail with his merchant ships and Queen Asla went back to her room with a heavy heart.

At first the merchant ships had good wind, but then a storm blew up, and the waves rose high, and drove them fast along the sea. They drove them into the trap of the tides along the coast of England, just as Queen Asla had said. They drove them to and fro, and at last they threw them on the grim rocks.

All three ships went down, and many Danes died. But King Goatskin, with some of his men, got safe to land. For no flood was able to drown him while he wore the magic shirt.

Then the Danish horns blew; and Danish hands let loose both fire and sword. They laid waste to everything. And the men of those parts fled to their king, King Ella, to tell him that men of war were in the land. King Ella sent word all round his kingdom, and came to meet King Goatskin with his English warriors.

Many arrows were aloft in the air that day. Many spears flew; many swords swung; many shields were broken; many helmets split. King Goatskin's Vikings fell fast around him. At last only King Goatskin was still standing, for the magic shirt kept him safe from sword and spear.

Then a band of English men attacked him, and carried him away. They bound him, and took him to King Ella.

King Ella was a cruel man, grim, big and black. He sat on a tall black horse that was shod with brass. He saw the rich chain mail King Goatskin wore, his wide golden arm rings, and the gold on his shield and his helmet. And he said to himself, *"Have I captured some Viking king?"* To Goatskin he said, with a roar like that of a bull, "What is your name, in your land?"

King Goatskin held his eyes with his, and said nothing.

Again King Ella gave his bull's roar. "Tell me, or you will have the worst death possible."

"I was not born to run away," said King Goatskin. And it came into his mind that this was what he had said to Tora Hart's dragon.

"Your name, your name!" cried King Ella. "Or I'll enjoy your death the worse it is."

"All men only die once," said King Goatskin. "No one shall mock my sons that their father was afraid of death."

King Ella put up his hand to stroke his black bush of a beard. "Will you crow as loud," he asked, "if I cast you into my snake pit?"

"When I was a boy," said King Goatskin, "I swore never to fear fire or sword or deep or dragon. I have kept that promise all my life. Should I not keep it, now I am old?"

"Bind his hands," said King Ella to his men, "and cast him in."

20. The Death Of Ragnar Goatskin

So the hands of King Goatskin were bound tight; and he was cast into the pit. Many snakes lay there, but the magic shirt kept him safe from them. He sang to them, and sang with such power that they all fell fast asleep.

All day long he lay in the pit, and sang the story of his life:

> *We struck with swords.*
> *While I was still a boy,*
> *I slew the Gothic dragon,*
> *And won white Tora Hart*
> *And my nickname, Goatskin.*
> *We struck with swords.*
> *I was young when, in the East,*
> *Hard iron sang on helmets.*
> *I carried my spear high*
> *When I was twenty years old,*
> *And took seven kings in one battle.*
> *We struck with swords.*

Loud was the din of battle.
The blue steel bit the golden mail.
The darts flew like dragons.
Golden was the reward.

King Ella rode his horse to the edge of the pit, to hear the song. His mother, Queen Grimhild, came too. She was a witch with a grim heart. "Do you know yet who he is?" she asked.

"King Ragnar of Denmark," he told her. "He spoke his nickname just now in his death song. If it is his death song. For he seems in no hurry to die."

"I cannot think of you as wise," she said, "if you cannot bring this man to his end."

"Tell me how," said King Ella.

"If he wears a magic shirt," said Queen Grimhild, "no snake can harm him. Strip him, and see."

So King Goatskin was drawn up out of the pit, and his magic shirt was torn off his back. But when he was cast back, the snakes still did not harm him. For he still sang on, and powerful words were in his song:

We struck with swords.
O, that the sons of Asla
Knew the fate of their father!
Wind swift would they be here!
Stark war would they wage on Ella!
For I gave to my sons a mother
Who gave them Sigurd hearts.

"I have torn his magic shirt from him," said King Ella, "yet still the snakes do not harm him."

"I see this is a matter for me, my son," said Queen Grimhild.

Now Queen Grimhild had skill in witchcraft. Like Princess Sibilya, she was a shape-shifter, able to take the form of any bird or beast. She took on the shape of an adder, crept into the pit, bit King Goatskin, and struck his heart.

But still King Goatskin sang on:

> *We struck with swords.*
> *I have won battles fifty-and-one.*
> *Now the snake finds my heart.*
> *Now the high gods make me a feast.*
> *Now the high gods call me home.*
> *The shield maids come to fetch me.*
> *They burn like flames in the sky.*
> *I shall drink full wine cups among the gods.*
> *The hours of my life here are spent.*
> *I die with laughter in my mouth."*

And so he died, with laughter in his mouth.

21. IVAR LACKBONES
FOUNDS LONDON

No news had come to Ledra of King Goatskin. Queen Asla went out, and sat down on the bench outside her window. Her three magpies flew to her.

"What news?" she asked them.

"Your Viking sons are sailing home," said the first.

"Send for your other sons," said the second. "For you will soon need them."

"Do you mean the King is dead?" cried Queen Asla. "How can that be, when he has my magic shirt to keep him safe?"

"If a fate is meant to be," said the third, as Kalf the Wiseman had said to King Herrad, "it will be, whatever you do."

So Queen Asla, with a heavy heart, sent for her sons, Born, King of Sweden, and White-Sark, King of Wendland, to come to her. And at the same time Ivar Lackbones and Sigurd Snake-in-the-Eye came back from their raid, with many riches.

As soon as news came to King Ella that King Goatskin's four sons were at Ledra, he sent a trusted man to tell them about their father's death.

"Watch carefully what they say and do when they hear the news," he told him. "Then come back and tell me."

The four brothers were in the hall when King Ella's man came in. King White-Sark and Ivar Lackbones sat playing chess. King Born Ironsides stood by them, making a spear shaft. Sigurd Snake-in-the-Eye sat near, cutting his fingernails.

"Lords," said King Ella's man, "I bring you news of the death of King Ragnar. He died in England, in King Ella's snake pit."

He saw King Born snap the spear shaft in two. He saw King White-Sark crush the chesspiece in his hand till blood sprang from under his nails. He saw Sigurd Snake-in-the-Eye cut his finger to the bone. But Ivar Lackbones sat still. Only his face went from white to red, and back again to white.

When King Ella's man went back to England and told King Ella this, King Ella said, "It is Ivar Lackbones then that we need to fear."

Queen Asla came down from her room. Her sons broke to her the news of King Goatskin's death. She went as white as someone who has died.

"O, I wish that he had never gone to England!" she cried. "O, I wish that I had kept him at home! I don't love life any more without him." And she went back to her room, and wasn't seen again that day.

Then Ivar Lackbones and Sigurd Snake-in-the-Eye cast lots as to who was to be King of Denmark in their father's place. Sigurd Snake-in-the-Eye was chosen.

Then the four brothers sat down to plan.

In those days, if a man was killed, there were two things his sons could do. They could go to war and take life for life, or they could take 'weregild', which was gold or land given to pay for the life taken.

The three kings, White-Sark and Born Ironsides and Sigurd Snake-in-the-Eye, chose the first way. Ivar Lackbones chose the second way.

"King Ella shall pay for our father's life," the three kings said, "with his own life, and with England, too."

"You three go to war with King Ella, if you want," said Ivar Lackbones. " I will go to him in peace, and ask for a bit of England as my weregild."

So the three kings got a great army ready to sail, to make war on England. Their sails blew out and their shieldwalls rang as their longships sped over the sea. They reached England on a late tide. When they reached land, they secured their ships in the mouth of a river, and waited there till dawn.

But King Ella had set men along the coast, to watch for them. These men told him, "Lord, three of the Danish sea princes have come, with so many ships our harbour will not hold them."

Then King Ella came with a great army of his own. The horns blew for battle; the Danes came rushing from their ships and their three kings shouted a war cry, to urge them on to the fight.

But the English army was too mighty for the Danes. Many were killed, and there were so many English warriors that the three kings saw they could never win that battle. They were glad to retreat to the ships with the Danes who were left, and to sail away with their lives.

Ivar Lackbones had had no part in that fight. As soon as the dragon ships sailed into Ledra, he himself set sail for England. His men carried him on his shield into the hall of King Ella.

"I come in peace, not war," he told King Ella, "to ask for weregild for my father."

"What weregild to you ask?" said King Ella.

"As much land as the skin of a horse will cover," Ivar Lackbones told him.

"What will you do with the land?" King Ella asked.

"I will live on it," said Ivar Lackbones. "There is no place for me in Ledra, now my brother Sigurd is king."

"Will you swear never to bear arms against me?" asked King Ella.

"I will swear that gladly," said Ivar Lackbones.

King Ella put up his hand to stroke his black bushy beard. *"I said that this was the son we had to fear,"* he said to himself. *"I was wrong. He has not a drop of his father's Viking blood in him."* And aloud he said, "You're asking for small weregild, for so mighty a king. Take it, and let it be a pledge of peace between us."

So Ivar Lackbones went away and got his horse skin. He cleverly cut it into strips so thin that they were as fine as hairs, and with them, he was able to enclose a vast area of land. He built his hall on the land, he gave it the name of 'Lunduna'. The city that stands there today with the same name: London.

Here Ivar Lackbones lived, at peace with King Ella. He saw how the English were ground down by their grim king. But his own fame went far and wide in King Ella's land of East England. No one in all the land had such a name for foresight and for farsight, and for being just and wise.

One day the chief men of King Ella's court came to Ivar Lackbones' hall. "Lord," they said, "the land of East England groans under our grim king and his grim mother.

It plots to rise against him. Will you aid us now, and be our king when it is all over?"

Ivar Lackbones sat on his high seat, and let this matter play to and fro in his mind. "I myself have sworn not to bear arms against King Ella," he said. "But I am free to send word to my brothers of how things are here. And when it is all over, you are still free to seek some other king, if that is your wish."

"It will not be," they said. "In all the seven kingdoms of England there is no man as wise and just as you."

So Ivar Lackbones sent word to his three brothers, the kings of the Swedes and the Danes and the Wends, to tell them how things were in East England. And the three kings came with a mighty army to help the English rise up against their king. King Ella died in that battle, and Queen Grimhild died with her son. The English made Ivar Lackbones their king, and he was a wise and just king till his death.

Only Princess Bleya was left from King Ella's family, and she was as good as King Ella and Queen Grimhild had been evil. Sigurd Snake-in-the-Eye, King of Denmark, fell in love with her, and made her his queen. And from them, and so from Asla, and so from Sigurd the Dragon Slayer, came many later kings and queens of Denmark and of England.

This is how the story ends:

> *Sigurd was the North's best helper;*
> *And after Sigurd,*
> *Ragnar was the first and best of men.*
> *Asla gave her five sons Sigurd hearts.*
> *Tora was above all other women*
> *As the hart is above all other wild things,*
> *As the sun is above the other lights of heaven.*

May this tale bring you
Wisdom in counsel,
Strength to meet danger,
Joy to meet sadness.

The Dream of King Alfdan

An Old Norse Hero Tale

CONTENTS

1. How Haki Was Made a Wolf's Head

King Sigurd the Hart was king of Ringrik in Norway. At the birth of his son he held a splendid feast. At the feast, King Sigurd sat in his high seat, and the newborn prince was laid at his feet. And King Sigurd gave the boy the name of Guthorm.

To this birth feast came the two kings of the lands next to Ringrik. They sat next to King Sigurd, at the top of the long table that ran the length of the hall. Next to the kings sat lords, in red furs and gold arm rings. And next to the lords sat the men, in coats of mail.

The lords drank lots of wine from golden wine cups. The men drank lots of ale, from ale horns bound with silver. And the king's hall rang with songs and jokes and laughter. Soon men who had drunk too much began to sprawl and to brawl. They began to shout and to brag, and to pluck at their daggers and sword hilts.

Ragnild, the new prince's sister, came in to bring the king's wine in a special cup. She was only six years old, but even then she had the nickname of Ragnild the Golden, because her hair was such a rich gold colour.

She gave the special cup first to the king next to her

father. This was the young king Alfdan the Black. As he drank from it, she lifted her head to gaze at his black hair.

"I've never seen black hair before," she said. "In Ringrik, our hair is golden."

"Ah," said King Alfdan the Black, "but I have a golden roof, the only one in all Norway. My hall is by a lake, and in the sun you can see its roof flash like gold fire over the water."

"My father's grave mound will be by a lake," said the little princess. "A wise man told him that it must be by a lake, and that it might help me in my hour of need."

King Alfdan gave her back the special cup. She gave it to the next king, King Eric the Merry. King Eric had red hair and his eyes were full of fun.

"What roofs do kings with red hair have?" asked the little princess.

"Roofs of straw, that birds can nest in," King Eric told her. "And the birds sing, to tell the kings with red hair things what will happen."

King Eric was joking, but what he said was true. He had a special gift of seeing into the future, and it was when the birds sang in his hall thatch that the gift was strongest.

"What do the birds sing about King Alfdan?" asked the little princess.

"They sing," said King Eric, "that he will dream a dream in a pigsty. The dream will only be a dream about his own hair, but it will signify a new fate for all of Norway."

"What do the birds sing about me?" asked the little princess.

"They sing," said King Eric, "that you will help to make that dream in the pigsty come true."

"What do the birds sing about you?" asked the little princess.

"They sing," said Eric, "that I, and this newborn Prince Guthorm, and that small boy who peeps in at the door, will all help to make the dream in the pigsty come true."

The little princess swept round to look at the boy at the door. "That's Koll," she said. "He's my friend. The lord next to you is his father, and the lord next to him is the father of those two big boys with Koll. They are Arek and Askel, they are my friends, too. Will they help the dream in the pigsty to come true?"

"The birds didn't say so," said King Eric, "so I don't think they will."

Koll's father shook the arm of the father of Arek and Askel. His face was red from drinking too much wine. "Did you hear that, Haki?" he cried. "My son will play a part in Norway's fate, but your sons will not."

"What did you say?" cried Haki, red with rage. And in a flash his sword was out and he killed Koll's father with one stroke.

A hush fell on the hall. All eyes were on King Sigurd.

With a deep sigh, King Sigurd rose from his high seat. "Haki," he said, "in one flash of rage you have robbed me of two good lords. For you know the law: because of that sword stroke, I must make you a wolf's head."

Little princess Ragnild asked King Eric, in a low voice, "What's a wolf's head?"

King Eric bent down and whispered in her ear. "An

outlaw. He must give up his hall and his lands and all that is his. He has three days of grace, then anyone who sees him will be free to kill him."

"Poor Haki!" said Ragnild the Golden. "What can he do?"

"All he can do," said King Eric, "is to run away from the parts of the land where people live. He must find a place to live, in some wild part where men do not go."

And this was what Haki the Wolf's Head did. When Haki fled, little princess Ragnild lost two of her friends because Haki's wife, his two young sons and his men went with him. They rode to a wild part of Ringrik, a part too wild for most men to live in. It was full of crags and cliffs, with no greenery. In it they came to a wide cleft in the cliffs. From the foot of the steep cliffs, far, far below, came the rush and roar of swift water.

"On the far side of a cleft like this," said Haki the Wolf's Head, "even a wolf's head will be safe." It was too wide a gap for a man to leap on foot, but it was not too wide for a good horse. So over the cleft, from cliff top to cliff top, one by one, sprang Haki's band on their horses. Then on they rode, till they came to a thick fir wood. And on among the fir trees they rode, till they came to a vast lake, deep in the wood.

"We will live in this wood," said Hald the Wolf's Head. "On this side the lake will protect us, and on that side the steep cleft."

"Father," said Arek, "let's set a trip cord on our side of the cleft. Then if a horse springs over, the cord will jolt it as it lands. And that will cast its rider over the cliff into the river far below."

"No man who doesn't need to will try to cross that cleft," said Haki. "All the same, my son, we will set a trip cord.

And it shall be yours, Arek, to look after." So a trip cord was set. And each day Arek went to see that it had not been sprung.

Soon Haki the Wolf s Head had a new hall, hidden deep in the fir wood. It was not as fine a hall as his old one, but it had a private room for his wife, and that room had an inner room for her two young sons.

When Arek and Askel grew older, they left this inner room and went to sleep with the men. Then Haki's wife used the inner room to dry her herbs. For this she needed a stream of air, so the men made her a round hole, high in the wall. The old Norse name for such an air hole was a "wind's eye".

Haki's wife used the herbs to heal the sick, for she was the healer in that hall of outlaws. When one of Haki's men was sick or hurt, he came to her to heal him. She was very skillful, as a lord's wives were in those days.

Arek spent much time with his father, but Askel spent much time with his mother. She saw, as he grew, that Askel had a love of herbs. So she taught him her skill, so that he could take her place as healer to the outlaws when she died.

From time to time, Haki and his outlaws went over the cleft at night. To the rich parts of Ringrik they rode, to rob and to raid. They soon had good store of gold and belongings. But they were so crafty and skillful in their raids that no one was able to track them back to the hall in the fir wood.

2. How King Sigurd Came to the Outlaws

Ten years went by. Haki's wife died, and Arek and Askel began to grow up. In all that time, no boat came over the lake. In all that time, no horse sprang over the cleft. In all that time, no man in all Ringrik found Haki's hall in the wilds.

Then, one day at the end of the fall, King Sigurd rode out alone to hunt the stag. He enjoyed hunting so much that his nickname was Sigurd the Hart.

He had not ridden far when a tall stag ran by. He set off after it. The stag was swift, and so was King Sigurd's horse. The stag raced over hill and dale, and King Sigurd raced over hill and dale.

By dusk, the stag had led him into a part of his land he did not know. All around him were vast crags and steep cliffs, with no greenery.

The stag came to a wide, deep cleft in the cliffs. From the foot of the cliffs, far, far below, came the rush and roar of swift water. Over the cleft, from cliff top to cliff top, sprang the stag. Over the cleft, from cliff top to cliff top, sprang King Sigurd on his horse.

Across the far cliff top, a trip cord ran. The stag sprang clear of it but King Sigurd's horse sprang into it. So sudden and sharp was the jolt that the king was thrown off his horse. His head hit the crag as he fell and he hung over the steep cleft, his left foot still held in its stirrup.

The king lay still, and his horse stood still beside him. Then, with slow steps, the horse began to drag the king away from the cleft. Its hoof took the trip cord with it. The horse went on till it came to a thick fir wood.

By now it was dark. Soon the full moon came up. Further on in the moonlit dark went the horse, deep into the wood. Far in the wood, hidden among the thick fir trees, the horse came to a hall. The horse stopped at the door of the hall, which was shut. On it, with its hard front hoof, the horse gave three raps, loud and sharp.

Haki the Wolf's Head and his outlaws sat in the hall, eating meat. Burning pine torches along the walls cast a red glow on silver dishes and golden wine cups from the outlaws' raids. At the sound of those three raps, the men sat still, ale horn in hand. Everyone looked at the door.

"Our first guest in all our ten years here!" cried Haki. "Ten men to the door, and let's see this night guest!" The ten men next to the door rose from the table. They went to the door and slid back the bar that held it fast. All ten stood sword in hand as the door swung gently open.

From moonlit night to torchlit hall, with slow steps, King Sigurd's horse came in. By the foot still held in the stirrup, it pulled the fallen king after it.

The men sprang up from the table, but Haki cried down the hall, "Everyone stay where they are! Let Askel look after this man first!"

Askel knelt by the king. He felt the king's head, his wrist, his brow. He laid his ear to the king's chest and to the king's lips. Then he stood up. "Father," he said, "this man is not yet dead. But he is so badly injured, he will die in three days' time. It seems he fell from his horse and broke his skull in the fall."

"It must have been at the cleft," said Arek, "because I can see my trip cord on the horse's hoof."

"But why did he come to the cleft?" asked Haki. "I don't think it was to seek us out, for it is a long time since our last raid."

"It may be that a stag led him," said Askel, "for he is dressed for the hunt. And yet he is no simple hunter. He has the look of a man of good birth."

At this, Haki rose and came down the hall. He bent low over the king. In the dim red glow, it was hard to see him clearly.

"Bring me a torch!" cried Haki. Arek ran to him with a lit pine torch. He held it to the king's face.

"He certainly is a man of good birth," said Haki. "I know this face well, even after ten years. I was his lord before he made me a wolf's head. This is King Sigurd the Hart!"

The name flew from lip to lip. All down the long bench a hubbub broke out.

"If he is so near his death hour, who will rule Ringrik next? For Prince Guthorm is only ten years old."

"Ragnild the Golden is sixteen. She is old enough to rule."

"But king's men want to be led by a king."

"Well, is she not old enough to get married? The man who marries her will be king."

"Some man will be lucky, then."

"Why not our Lord Haki?"

At that, one and all took up the cry: "Let Lord Haki marry Ragnild the Golden! And let us all be king's men!"

Haki the Wolf's Head held up his hand. A hush fell. "First things first," said Haki. "Askel, take four men and carry the king to a bed. Treat his injuries, and stay at his side." Four men rose from the bench and came to King Sigurd. They lifted him up and carried him from the hall. Askel the Healer went with them.

Then, with bent head, Haki trod the length of his hall, to and fro. To and fro, the eyes of his men went with him. In that long hall, the only sound was the tramp of Haki's feet.

Then he stood still. He lifted up his head. "This plan you fill my ears with is a bold plan, men," he cried. "We shall need to think it out carefully. But we will try it!"

Back on his high seat, chin in hand, Haki made his plans, with Arek at his side to help him. "The king's men won't be worried about the king yet," said Haki. "I remember that he often spends the night outdoors, if the hunt takes him far away."

"And I remember," said Arek, "that when he did this, it was often Ragnild who would ride out alone, the next day at dawn, to meet him."

"Then she plays into our hands," cried Haki. "We can whisk her away as she rides out at dawn and be back for the wedding feast by sunset."

"We must take Prince Guthorm, too," said Arek, "so that, with the princess gone, the king's men can't make him king."

"When King Sigurd dies," said Haki, "the king's men will not know it. The first they will know of it will be when Queen Ragnild rides into her hall, with King Haki at her side. So we do not need to take Prince Guthorm, if he is not with her. But if he is with her, it would be best to take him too."

"Will you bring her by force, or coax her, or hoax her?" asked Arek.

"We will give her the true news that the king lies close to death," said Haki. "I think that then she will come of her own free will. Now, Askel shall stay to look after the king, and a third of the men shall stay to decorate the hall for the wedding feast. Tell the rest to bring out the horses. We must be on our way in an hour if we are to meet my bride at dawn!"

3. How the Outlaws Took Ragnild the Golden

At dawn the next day, Ragnild the Golden rode out from the king's hall to meet her father. She had grown tall and fair of face, and her hair was still as rich a gold as when she was a child.

"I will ride with you, sister," said little prince Guthorm. "You need a man to guard you, now you are old enough to get married."

Koll, Princess Ragnild's old friend, was now King Sigurd's page. "A ten-year-old shrimp of a lad is no guard for a golden princess," said Koll. "I think I had better come too, and guard you both."

So all three set off at dawn. Out they rode, among fields that had been full of ripe corn a few weeks ago. On they rode, across the green vale that fed the cows. And so they came to a bright wood of silver birch trees.

As they rode in the wood, Ragnild the Golden held back her horse. "Do you hear hoofbeats?" she asked. *Thud, thud, thud*, came the beat of hoofs from far away.

"I know that hoofbeat," said little prince Guthorm. "It is our father's horse. How fast he rides home today!" *Thud, thud, thud*, came the hoofbeats, loud and louder, near and nearer. Then into sight, among the silver birch trees, came a horse.

"Yes," said Ragnild the Golden, "that is our father's horse. But is that our father on it?"

"It is not," said Koll. "It is someone I have never seen. And yet it seems to me that it is someone I have seen before, long ago."

As the rider came near to them, he drew his horse up sharp. "Princess Ragnild!" he cried, "I come to you from King Sigurd the Hart. You will recognise this horse as his. And he sends you his ring." He held out a ring to her.

"What has happened to my father?" cried Ragnild. "Yes, yes, this is his horse, and this is his ring."

"He fell from his horse and is badly hurt," said the rider. "He lies now at my hall. I've come to take you to him."

"Koll," said the princess, "ride back and bring men to carry my father home. My brother and I will ride on with you, my lord. How is it that I don't know your face or name?"

Koll frowned as he swung around his horse to ride back to the hall. He felt that he knew that man. And he felt that he did not trust him. And then it came to him who it was. He knew that face from when he was a child, ten years ago. It was the face of the man who had killed his father.

"It is Haki the Wolf's Head!" he cried. He flung his dagger at Haki. It pierced Haki's chainmail and went deep into his side. Then, from among the birch trees, came horse after horse, each with its rider dressed in chainmail, spear in hand and sword at side. Amid that sudden throng of men, the prince and princess did not see the spear flung towards Koll. They did not see Koll fall.

One rider cried, as he rode to Haki's side, "Father, are you hurt?"

"I can last till Askel can heal me, Arek," said Haki.

"Arek!" cried Ragnild the Golden. "If what your father said about my father is true, why have you come to fetch me with spears?"

"What my father tells you is true, Princess Ragnild," said Arek. "It is only with spears that we *can* come, for remember that we are outlaws. All men are free to kill us at sight, as you saw Koll try to kill my father. Each of us risks his life, Princess, to bring you to the king."

Ragnild the Golden bit her lip and bent her head, for she saw that this was true. "You are right," she said. "And I owe you all a lot. Now let us ride to my father."

At a swift pace the throng of men set off, with the prince and princess in the midst of them. By secret byways they cut across the land to the wild, bare tract of crags and cliffs. They did not stop till they came to the wide, deep cleft, with its rush and roar of swift water far below.

"It was at this cleft that the king your father fell, Princess," said Arek. "Shall I tie you to your horse for the leap across?"

"No," said Ragnild the Golden, "I can sit strong on my horse."

"Shall I tie *you* to your horse, Prince?" asked Arek.

"No," said little prince Guthorm. "I can sit strong on my horse."

"Tie me, my son," said Haki, with a gasp. "For I am weak from loss of blood."

Arek bound his father to King Sigurd's horse. Over the wide cleft, from cliff top to cliff top, one by one, sprang the horses.

"Do not untie me, Arek, in case I fall," said Haki, his hand to his side. "Set up the trip cord when the last horse is over."

Arek did. Then on and into the fir wood they rode and they came to Haki's hidden hall. Cries and shouts of joy

met them at the door of the hall. But the joy was cut short when the men who ran out saw Haki drooping on his horse. He was so weak now that his men had to lift him down and carry him into the hall.

"Carry me to my bed, men," said Haki. "Arek, bring our guests to the king. And send Askel to me. Tell him I have need of his skill."

Prince Guthorm's eyes were wide as he was led into the hall. For its long table was set with gold and silver, as if for a feast, and a blaze of gold cloth lay on the long bench and on the high seat.

Across fresh straw, Arek led the prince and princess to his mother's room. "It was my mother's way, when one of us was sick," he told them, "to look after him in her room. So it is in her room, that is now *your* room, Princess, that we have laid the king."

As they came into the room, Askel the Healer rose from his seat by the king's bed. Ragnild the Golden ran to meet him.

"Askel, how is my father?" she cried.

Askel bent low over her hands. "Princess, he sleeps. He can only last a short time now," he said.

Ragnild laid her hand on her father's brow, then sank into Askel's seat. Here she sat, as still as the still shape on the bed, till Arek came in with a silver bowl of water. He knelt to wash the hands and feet of his guests, as was the way in the old days.

"That chest holds all my mother's belongings, Princess," he said. "Take from it what you need. This inner room is yours, Prince. It was mine and Askel's when we were boys, and the chest in it is full of our belongings from when we, too, were ten years old. Take what you need."

"My father's death is not far off," said Ragnild the Golden. "So don't set a place for me in the hall, Arek. I will stay with him till the end."

"As you wish, Princess," said Arek. And to himself he said, *"Since the wedding feast must be put off."* For as soon as Askel had seen the wound in Haki's side, he had told him, "Father, with this gash in your side you will hold no wedding feast tonight, nor for many nights yet."

"No matter, as long as I hold it in the end," said Haki. "Koll has delayed the wedding feast. But Ringrik's new queen is still mine."

4. How Princess Ragnild Saw the Golden Roof

That night, as the princess sat at his side, King Sigurd the Hart died in his sleep. Ragnild the Golden wept over him. Then she took the king's ring and placed it on Prince Guthorm's thumb.

"You are king of Ringrik now, little brother," she told him.

But Prince Guthorm pulled the big ring off his thumb and gave it back to her. "Wear it for me, Ragnild," he said. "I am too small yet to be a king. Koll calls me just a ten-year-old shrimp of a lad, and Koll is right."

"What has happened to Koll? He's taking so long to bring our father's men" said Ragnild. "We need them now to seek a lake, and to make our father's grave mound at its side."

But when she said this to Arek, he told her, "Princess, a lake lies but a stone's throw from this hall. Our men will make the king's grave mound at its side for you."

"Take me to this lake," said Ragnild the Golden, "so that I can find the right place for my father's bones to rest."

"Then come with me now," said Arek. "At this dawn hour our men go to the lake to collect water." So out into the dawn went the princess and the little prince, with Arek and the men with the water holders. Two by two they went along the track among the fir trees, the track that led away from the cleft.

Soon they came to the end of the track. To the left and to the right stood the wild, thick wood. And in front of them lay a lake so vast that it was water, water, all the way to the far sky.

Along the bank the men spread out, to fill the water holders. Ragnild the Golden went to and fro at the lakeside with slow steps and bent head, till she knew she had found the place for her father's grave mound.

"Let it be here," she said.

In Ragnild's room, King Sigurd the Hart lay in state. And at the lakeside, Haki's men cut down fir trees and made a round room in the ground for King Sigurd the Hart to sit in, with gold and belongings, and with sword and shield, and with all that a king in the old days took with him to his grave.

Koll and the king's men still hadn't come to the hall in the wilds, so it was Haki's men who placed King Sigurd the Hart in the round room, and over it made a mound, wide and high, to mark the grave of a king.

Then Ragnild the Golden said to Arek, "Now that my father is laid to rest, I must go back to his hall with my brother, so that he can be made king. And his first act as king shall be to give Lord Haki his lands back, and to freely pardon everyone in this hall."

But Arek said, "Princess, it is not my father's will that your brother be made king. He wants you be queen. He wants you to stay here till he is well, and then he wants to marry you."

"Haki wants to marry me?" cried Ragnild the Golden. "Has Koll's dagger sent him mad?" She swung round in rage, swept into her room, and shut the door with a bang.

Little prince Guthorm came out from the inner room. He came with a slip and a slide, for he had boy's ice skates on his feet. "Look, Ragnild!" he cried. "I found skates that fit me in Arek's chest. They must have been his when he was my age. Ragnild! Why are you in such a rage?"

Then Ragnild sank into a seat and pulled him to her, and told him everything that Arek had said.

As he sat and took off the skates, Guthorm said, "I think this plot must have been in Haki's mind from the start, for as we came into the hall, I saw that it was laid for a feast. I think it would have been your wedding feast, Ragnild, had Koll's dagger not delayed it."

"How can Haki dream he can make me marry him," cried Ragnild, "when he knows Koll is on his way to us with a band of our father's men?"

"But is Koll on the way?" asked Prince Guthorm. "If this plot was in Haki's mind from the first, then he left no men in the birch wood to guide our men to this hall. If this plot was in Haki's mind, it may be that he had Koll killed, so that now our own men have no clue as to what happened to us."

"If what King Eric said at your birth feast was true," said Ragnild, "Koll cannot be dead. For Koll was to help to make the dream in the pigsty come true."

"It is Koll who has put off the wedding feast," said Guthorm. "It may be that that was his help. Our men must have ridden far and wide by now to seek us, Ragnild, but I think this hall is too well hidden for them ever to find it. Should we not try to slip out and find our own way back?"

"The door of my room is our only way out," said Ragnild. "Go, Guthorm, and try that door. I fear you will find that a bar has been set across it."

The little prince set down the skates and ran to try the door. A bar on the far side held it fast. "You are right, Ragnild," he said. "We can't go that way. But my room has a wind's eye. If we can get up to it, we can slip out there."

"We can, if you have a spell to make me as small as you, little brother," said Ragnild with a sad smile. "I am far too big as I am to slip out of a wind's eye."

"Then I will go," said Guthorm, "and bring our men back to free you."

"And will you fly across the cleft to fetch them?" asked Ragnild, with her sad smile.

"No, I will steal a horse from the stable," said the little prince.

"First you must put the stablemen to sleep," said Ragnild.

Then little prince Guthorm said, "If we can't find a way to cross that cleft, we must try the other way."

"And how will you cross the lake?" asked Ragnild. "I didn't see a boat by the bank. Will you grow wings?"

A flick of Prince Guthorm's hand swept aside the skates, and they fell with a clang. "Ragnild!" he cried. "It is the end of the fall. In a week or two we shall see ice on the lake. Then I won't need a boat or wings, I can cross on Arek's ice skates!"

Ragnild the Golden bent and gave him a hug. "Ah, if only we knew what is on the far side!" she said with a sigh. "It may well be a wild land, as this is, too wild for good men to live in."

Prince Guthorm sat at her feet, his chin in his small hand. He was still for a time. "Ragnild," he said at last, "tell me again what the wise man told our father about his grave mound."

"He told him," said Ragnild, "that it must be at the side of a lake, so that it might help me in my hour of need."

"Then seek its help," said the little prince. "For it seems that this is your hour of need."

When it was time to eat, the door of the room swung open and men came in with rich food in a golden dish and wine in golden wine cups.

As Princess Ragnild took the food, she said to them, "Tell Lord Arek it is my wish, when next you go to collect water, to go with you to my father's grave to pray."

"We will tell him, Princess," said the men.

So again the prince and the princess went out into the wood with Arek and the men with the water holders. Two by two they went along the track among the fir trees. But with them this time, in front and at the back, went men with spears. When they came to the lake, the men spread along the bank to collect water.

"I will go to the top of the mound alone," said Princess Ragnild. "My brother will stay here with you, below."

The men with the spears stood around the foot of the mound. With slow steps and bent head, Ragnild the Golden went up its slope. She came to the crest, and sat down to look around her. It was as if she sat on the top of a small hill.

She let her mind grow still, so that if any help came, she would hear it. As she sat, looking on the water, the sun came out. And far away in front of her, she saw a flash of gold. "What can that be?" she asked herself. "It came like a flash of golden fire over the water."

And then her mind went back ten years. She saw her father's hall at the newborn Guthorm's birth feast. She saw herself, a small princess six years old, come in with the golden cup. She saw herself give the special cup to a king with black hair.

"I've never seen black hair before," said that small princess. "In Ringrik our hair is golden."

And what was it that the king with the black hair had said back to her? Her eyes grew bright as it all came back, "Ah, but I have a golden roof, the only one in all Norway. My hall is by a lake, and in the sun you can see its roof flash like golden fire over the water."

So now she knew that King Alfdan of Hadland had his hall on the far side of the lake. She realised then that the outlaws did not know this. She realised that what she had seen was a secret. She realised that to see that flash you had to be high in the air, as she was on the crest of her father's grave mound. Down below, on the bank, you couldn't see the gold fire.

When Ragnild and Guthorm were in her room again, Guthorm asked, "Did our father's grave mound help in your hour of need, Ragnild?"

"It did, little brother," she told him. "I know now that everything will be well. For on the far side of the lake lives the king who is to dream the dream in the pigsty."

5. How Prince Guthorm Went for Help

Each night after that, when the prince and the princess were left alone and the bar held the door locked, they swept the straw away from part of the floor. Then, in the dust, Ragnild the Golden drew a map of the sky, to teach the little prince how to find his way across the lake with the help of the stars.

Each day the prince and the princess went to the lake with the men who went to collect water. When Ragnild had sent to say that this was her wish, Askel the Healer had said to Haki, "It is good to let them do this, Father, for at the king's hall the princess was out of doors a lot. If she doesn't get enough fresh air now, she may well fall sick. With Arek and the men about them, they cannot slip away."

Day by day it grew colder, till the day came when they went out to find snow in deep drifts on the track. And soon after this came the day when they stood on the bank of the lake and saw in front of them one vast sheet of ice.

That day Arek said, as they went back, "In three days, Askel tells me, our father can rise from his bed and hold his wedding feast. In three days, Princess, you will be my stepmother, and you, little Prince, my uncle!"

As soon as they were alone for the night, Ragnild the

Golden said, "It must be soon now, Guthorm, or we shall be too late."

"Let it be now," said the little prince. "It is a full moon, and that will help."

He took Arek's ice skates from the chest, and put on thick furs. Ragnild gave him a kiss and a hug. They placed a bench by the wall of the inner room, so that it stood under the wind's eye. They stood on the bench and Ragnild took him into her arms, to lift him to the wind's eye.

As she held him up, he was just able to stretch and reach to the high round hole. He was just able to cling and to hang from it by his hands.

"May Ull, the god of snowshoes, be with you, little brother," said Ragnild the Golden.

Prince Guthorm drew his small form up to the wind's eye. He got one foot out to the far side. Then he got both feet out to the far side. Out he went. Over he went. He hung and clung by his hands in the sharp night air.

Moss grew on the outer wall of the hall, and grass grew on the outer wall of the hall, so it was not hard for Guthorm to find footholds. It was not hard for him to find handholds. Inch by inch, down the wall, slid the little prince, till his foot felt the soft snow on the ground.

He crept into the moonlit fir wood. The footprints left by the men that day were black in the white snow. Along the track they led him, among the fir trees, to the lake. He stood on the bank of the lake, at the foot of his father's grave mound, and he drew in a deep, deep breath.

To the left and to the right he saw a long, long plain of ice stretch far away to melt into the distant dark. In front he saw a long, long plain of ice stretch far away, to melt into the distant dark.

He bent down, and bound his skates to his feet. He stood up and pulled his furs tightly around him. Then, as light as a bird, and as swift as a bird, he began to skim across that moonlit, misty, vast white plain of ice.

So fast he flew that his swift flight made a wind. Chill, chill, blew that wind. Even with Arek's furs about him, Guthorm felt the chill creep into his bones. So fast he flew, and so vast was the plain he flew over, that it began to seem as if he flew in a dream. The white light of the moon, the white mist, the white ice, all were like something in a dream.

So clear were the stars that he was able to match them with the map of the sky he had saved up in his mind, night by night. He was able to steer his path by them. So bright a light did the full moon give that, after a time, he was able to make out dim forms along the skyline, far in front of him.

On he flew, and he saw now that the dim, dark forms were trees. Still he flew on. The trees drew near; the trees grew clear. At last, in the long dark line of trees, he saw a gap. And in the gap he saw the light of the moon gleam on a roof, part white with snow, part bright with gold, that was set among the trees.

He was so happy that he sang out loud, "I have come across the lake from Ringrik to Hadland! I have found the hall with the golden roof of King Alfdan the Black!"

He reached the bank. Stiff and sore, he came up off the ice on to the snow. He unbound his skates and up the slope he went, and under the porch to the door of King Alfdan's hall.

He felt for the guest horn that hung at the side of the door. He set it to his lips and he blew a blast on it.

The door swung wide open. In from the moonlit night, with slow, stiff steps, went a small lad dressed in furs, a pair of skates in his hand.

A hush fell over the men about the fires as the lad went up the hall and stood in front of the high seat. On the high seat sat King Alfdan. So black was his hair that the lad lifted his head to gaze at it.

"I've never seen black hair before," he said. "In Ringrik our hair is golden."

"A small princess said the same to me ten years ago," said King Alfdan.

"That was at my birth feast," said the little prince. "I am Prince Guthorm of Ringrik. My father, King Sigurd the Hart, is dead. Haki the Wolf's Head holds my sister. In three days he wants to marry her, so that he may take the land for his own."

"You're swaying on your feet, Prince," said King Alfdan. "Sit, eat, and drink. Then tell me all your tale."

Stiff and sore, the little prince sat. He ate. He drank. He told the king all his tale. Then he went to sleep with his head in the dish.

Torlef, King Alfdan's wise man, said, "Let him sleep, lord. A grown man might well be worn out by what this lad has made his small self do tonight."

King Alfdan cried down the hall, "Let each man bring out his sledge, to cross the lake to Ringrik."

The little prince still slept as Torlef picked him up and carried him out to the king's sledge. "Let him sleep, lord," he said again. "We have no need of him yet. The marks of his skates on the ice will guide us over the lake."

And in Torlef's arms the little prince still slept as the sledge sped over the vast plain of ice, with three of King Alfdan's strong horses to pull it, as swift as black birds in the moonlight.

Not till the sledge drew up by King Sigurd's grave mound on the far bank of the lake did Torlef the Wise wake the lad. "We need your help now, Prince Guthorm," he told him. "Show us the way to Haki's hall."

They left a small band of men with the horses. The little prince led the rest along the track among the fir trees. All was still in Haki's hall. The outlaws slept soundly as King Alfdan broke in.

The fight was short and sharp. Outlaws fell to the left and to the right, as the little prince led Torlef the Wise to the door of the room, and slid back the bar.

"Ragnild! Ragnild!" he cried. Then he was with her. Her arms were about him. Her rich gold hair was about him.

With Torlef he led her out into the free air of the moonlit

night. He ran with her along the track to the lake. He put her in the king's sledge, as King Alfdan and his men came back to their sledges.

Then Haki the Wolf's Head rose up from his sickbed. He took up his sword and crept out to the stable. He found King Sigurd's horse. Down to the edge of the lake he rode, swaying in his saddle, his sword swaying in his hand.

They saw him looming up, black in the moonlight. They saw the horse slip as it set a hoof on the ice. They saw Haki thrown from his saddle, as Sigurd the Hart had been thrown. They saw Haki fall on his sword at the foot of King Sigurd's grave mound. He knew then that his death hour was upon him.

"You have won my princess from me, Alfdan the Black," he cried. "But when you reach the age that I am now, take heed. Take heed, in case ice brings you to your death then, as now it brings me to mine." And with that, he died.

"Lord," said Torlef the Wise to King Alfdan, "let us take this wolf's head with us, and give him a hero's grave. That way you may be freed from his death wish."

So they lifted up Haki and placed him in the sledge.

"How old was Haki, Guthorm?" asked King Alfdan.

"Forty years old," the little prince told him.

"Ah, then," cried King Alfdan, in a lively mood, "I have twice seven years to live till I need fear this icy fate!" Then back across the lake they went, to the hall with the golden roof.

6. THE QUEEN'S DREAM AND THE KING'S DREAM

When he got back to Hadland, King Alfdan the Black gave Haki the Wolf's Head a hero's grave. A round room was dug for him at the lakeside, south of the hall with the golden roof, by the Place of the Cattle Branding. A mound was made over it, to mark the grave of a hero.

The day after the flight across the ice, King Alfdan the Black got up at dawn to greet the sun. When he went to go out by the sunrise door of his hall, he found the bar drawn back. And when he went out, a golden princess stood by the wall, to greet the sun with him.

Then King Alfdan first saw clearly, after ten years, the princess he had sped over the ice to save. And Princess Ragnild first saw clearly, after ten years, the king who had crossed the ice to save her. Each fell in love with the other, and so, they were married.

As they sat at the wedding feast, little prince Guthorm came up the long hall to them. He stood in front of the high seat as he had stood the first time he had come to this hall with the golden roof.

"I bring you a vow as a wedding gift," he said.

"What vow is that, little brother?" asked the new Queen Ragnild.

The little prince said, "When I am a man, the land of Ringrik will be mine. But I vow never to be its king. I give it to you, Alfdan and Ragnild, to add to your own land of Hadland."

"That is a kingly wedding gift," said King Alfdan. "But why give us everything you have of your own?"

"For the sake of both lands," said the little prince. "For it seems to me that when two small lands each have a king, both lands are weak. But when two small lands have the same king, both lands are strong."

Then Torlef the Wise said, "This lad is small, but he is as wise as he is brave. This deed of his may well be the seed of a new fate for all of Norway."

So the little prince lived with King Alfdan and Queen Ragnild in the hall with the golden roof. So wise was he, and such skill did he show in swordcraft as he grew, that Torlef said to King Alfdan, "As soon as he is old enough to lead men, you will do well, lord, to place him above all your own men."

"This will we do," said King Alfdan, "on the day he is sixteen winters old."

So time went on, till Ragnild the Golden had been a queen for three years. Then, one night, she had a dream. In her dream, she stood in her garden. And as she stood, she felt the prick of a thorn. She felt for the thorn, and pulled it out of her dress. As she held the thorn in her hand, it began to grow. It grew at both ends. It grew up, it grew down. So much did it grow, so fast did it grow, that soon it had grown into a vast tree.

One end of the thorn went down among the grass. Deep, deep, into the ground it went, till the tree had long, firm roots. The other end of the thorn grew high in the air. The trunk grew thick. Far across the sky it spread long, strong twigs.

In her dream, Queen Ragnild saw that the roots of this vast tree were as red as blood. She saw that the trunk was as green as grass, and the twigs were as white as snow. So vast was the tree that from her garden that it spread out over all the long land of Norway.

At dawn, Queen Ragnild told this dream to King Alfdan. King Alfdan told it to Torlef the Wise, who had much skill in interpreting dreams.

"How do you read this dream, Torlef?" asked the king.

"I read it like this, lord," said Torlef. "From the queen shall spring a king who shall rule over all of Norway."

"That will be a royal fate," said King Alfdan. "But why are the roots of the tree as red as blood?"

Torlef the Wise said, "Lord, I take the tree to be a son the queen will give birth to. And I take the blood red roots to mean that in his first years, his root years as king, blood will be shed to make those roots strong and firm."

"And why a trunk as green as grass?" asked the king.

"I take the green trunk," said Torlef, "to mean that in this king's middle years, the land will be rich and bear good crops."

"And why is the top of the tree as white as snow?" asked King Alfdan.

"I take the snow white top," said Torlef, "to mean that this king will live to be very old, with hair as white as snow."

"Why do I not dream such dreams?" asked King Alfdan.

"It may be," said Torlef, "that you do not sleep in the right place for dreams. Didn't King Eric the Merry's birds sing of a dream in a pigsty? When I wish to dream, I go and sleep in my pigsty."

"Then so will I," said the king.

So that night, King Alfdan went to sleep in the pigsty. He lay on clean straw by the pigs. He slept, and in his sleep he had a dream.

In his dream, King Alfdan saw himself. He saw new locks of hair spring out of his head. Some grew down to his heel. Some grew to his shin. Some grew to his knee. Some grew to his hip. Some grew to his chest. Some grew to his neck. Some were only wisps that sprang out from the crown of his head. But one lock was so long that it grew right down to the ground.

Now King Alfdan's own hair was as black as night. But in his dream, only a few of his locks were black. Some were brown. Some were red. Most of them were golden. One lock was so fair that it stood out among the rest. It was as pale as flax. This flax-pale lock was the same lock that grew right down to the ground.

Next day at dawn, King Alfdan left the pigsty and stood at the sunrise door of his hall to greet the sun. Then he went to find Torlef the Wise and he told him his dream.

"How do you read this dream in the pigsty?" he asked.

"I read it like this," said Torlef, "that from you will spring a race of kings that shall rule the land with power."

"And the long locks and the short locks?" asked King Alfdan.

"As some of the locks were long and some short," said Torlef, "so some kings shall rule with more power and some with less."

"And the fair lock so long that it grew down to the ground?" asked King Alfdan.

"As that lock is longer than the rest," said Torlef, "that king shall rule with more power than the rest. From the queen's dream we know that he will be the first king to bring all Norway under his power, and that he will be your son."

"I long to meet this son! May he come soon!"

And soon he came. In less than a year, a son was born to King Alfdan and Queen Ragnild. The boy didn't have black hair like his father. Nor did he have gold hair, like his mother. His hair was so pale that it was as pale as flax.

They called him Harald. And from his flax-pale hair he got, even as a child, the nickname of Harald Fairhair.

King Alfdan was thirty years old when his son was born. The boy grew into a strong child, big, bold and brave, with skill in all sports. Everything went well till the winter when he was ten years old and his father, King Alfdan, was forty.

When the days grew cold at the end of the fall that year, Torlef the Wise said to King Alfdan, "Lord, take notice of the ice this winter. We gave Haki the Wolf's Head a hero's grave. This winter will show if that freed you from his death wish."

7. Who Stole the King's Yuletide Feast?

At the beginning of that winter, King Alfdan sent a branding iron to each farm and hall in Hadland. This was to bring the news that it was time to hold a cattle branding.

So, as soon as the ice had set on the lake, from all parts of the land men came to the Place of the Cattle Branding. And each man drove his cattle before him.

For the ten-year-old Prince Harald, this was a time of great fun. The plain of ice at the foot of Haki's grave mound was a mass of cattle, with wave upon wave of tall white horns riding on its crest. The air was loud with new sounds – the blare of bulls, the shouts of the cowherds, the ring of hoofs on the ice.

The little prince ran in and out among the cattle. He threw ropes to help hold them. He fed the fires with pine logs. He held branding irons in the flame to heat them. He sang songs round the fires with the cowherds.

Among the cowherds that year was a Finn. He was small and slight and dark. His name was Ross. No other cowherd told such tales as Ross the Finn. No other cowherd sang such songs as he did. He knew special chants that were able to call up mists and snow and winds, chants that were able to hide the sun, and chants to make a bare tree seem to be in full leaf. For in Norway, in the old days, it was believed that all Finns were troll-wise, and to be troll-wise was to have skill in witchcraft.

No other cowherd was as good with cattle as Ross the Finn. He knew how to heal a cow of all her illnesses. With him bulls were as tame as lambs. So, when the cattle branding was over, King Alfdan kept him on as one of his own cowherds.

From then on, Prince Harald spent all his time with Ross the Finn. No more did he come to his uncle, Prince Guthorm, to teach him swordcraft. No more did he come to Torlef the Wise, to teach him booklore. No more did he come to his father, King Alfdan, to teach him things of state. But every day he came to Ross the Finn, to teach him special chants, and songs, and how to skate, and how to ski.

Ross the Finn made Prince Harald snowshoes and skates of bone. They had a curl in front, like the prow of a ship. Ross the Finn spoke special chants over them.

"Now they will carry you to whatever place you want, little prince," said Ross the Finn.

Yuletide came round. In King Alfdan's hall the long table was set for the yuletide feast. The air was full of rich smells. Fires were ablaze the length of the hall. The walls were hung with gold cloth, the table was bright with the gleam of gems and of gold and of silver.

King Alfdan and Queen Ragnild sat on the high seat. Next to them sat Prince Guthorm and Torlef the Wise. But little prince Harald sat at the foot of the table, next to Ross the Finn.

And then, as the men sat down, and took up meat daggers, and put out hands to fill ale horns, all in the blink of an eye, the table was as bare as a bone. Meat and drink, dish and wine cup, gem and gold and silver, all disappeared into thin air.

"Witchcraft!" cried King Alfdan. And from lip to lip, all down the long table, flew the cry, "Witchcraft! Witchcraft!"

The eyes of everyone went to the small, dark man at the foot of the table – to the cowherd, Ross the Finn. King Alfdan sent a servant down the hall to tell Ross the Finn come to him.

Ross the Finn rose, and went up the hall, and stood in front of the high seat. Little prince Harald rose too and went up the hall with him. He also stood in front of the high seat.

King Alfdan was in a black mood. His black brows drew down over his black eyes. It was clear to see that it was not only from his black hair that he had got his nickname of Alfdan the Black.

"What hand have you had in this, Finn?" he cried.

"Lord, no hand at all," said Ross the Finn.

King Alfdan gave a shout of rage. "But you are troll-wise. In all this hall, Finn, only you are troll-wise. If you had no hand in it yourself, still only you can tell me who took the feast from my table."

"Lord, that is not mine to tell you," said Ross the Finn.

"You *shall* tell me, Finn!" cried King Alfdan.

Ross the Finn stood still in front of the high seat. His eyes met the eyes of the king. He made no sound.

"Take him," said King Alfdan to his servants. "Tie his hands and feet. Throw him into the cave room under the hall. Don't give him any meat, don't give him any drink, till he tells me who took the feast from my table."

"No, Father! No, no, no!" cried little prince Harald. And

he tried to cling to Ross the Finn. But King Alfdan set a strong hand on his son's arm as the servants took Ross the Finn away. They tied his hands and feet. They threw him into the cave room under the hall. They shut the cave room door and slid the bar to bolt him in.

Twice a day, King Alfdan went to the door of the cave room and asked Ross the Finn, "Who took the feast from my table?" And twice a day Ross the Finn told him, "Lord, that is not mine to tell you."

On the third day, when King Alfdan had left the hall, little prince Harald crept to the door of the cave room. "Ross, it is I, Harald," he said in a low tone.

"Help me, little prince!" said Ross the Finn, with a gasp. "Beg the king to let me have meat and drink, or I shall die."

Prince Harald ran after King Alfdan. He threw his arms around his father's knees. "Father, let Ross have meat and drink, I beg you," he cried. "If you do not, he will die."

"He shall have meat and drink," said King Alfdan the Black, "when he tells me who took the feast from my table."

Then in his mind little prince Harald made a vow, *"I shall give my Finn meat and drink!"*

That night Prince Harald got into his bed still dressed. When all was still, he rose. He stood at the door of his room and held his breath and listened. King Alfdan and all his men were deep asleep.

Prince Harald crept out to the hall. The pine torches along the walls had all burnt out, but a small red glow still came from the embers. By that small red glow he was able to see. Food from last night's meal lay still on the long table. Drink from last night's meal still stood on the long table. Prince Harald put a meat dagger in his belt, and took a full plate of meat and a full horn of ale in both hands.

He crept to the door of the cave room. "Ross, it is I, Harald," he said in a low tone.

He put down the dish and the ale horn, and slid back the bar that held the door locked. Into the cave room he crept.

Ross the Finn lay in the dark, bound hand and foot. The little prince felt him all over till he found his bonds. Then he drew the meat dagger from his belt and cut him free.

Then back he crept to the door, for the dish and the ale horn. Ross the Finn sat up and took them. In the dark he ate and drank, and was glad and full of thanks.

"If I let you out, Ross," said Prince Harald, "can you get safely away?"

"With skates I can," said Ross the Finn.

"Skates you shall have," said the little prince. "But do you have a secret place you can hide in from my father? I do not think any place in all Hadland will be safe if he stays in his black mood."

"I need not stay in Hadland," said Ross the Finn. "I can go south over the lake to King Eric the Merry in Ordland."

"Ah, good King Eric!" said Prince Harald with a sigh. "So good, so kind, so merry, no black moods. How lucky any boy would be to have such a father! I'd like to meet him."

"Then why not come with me to him now?" said Ross the Finn. "It will be hard with you if you are here when your father finds out you have set me free."

"Can a ten-year-old boy skate so far?" asked the little prince.

"Didn't a ten-year-old Prince Guthorm skate from Ringrik to Hadland?" said Ross the Finn. "Then can't a ten-year-old Prince Harald skate from Hadland to Ordland?"

"I will come with you, Ross," said Prince Harald. "Wait, while I fetch us skates and furs."

When he came back with the furs and the skates, Prince

Harald said, "Let's go out by the sunset door. That bar is less hard to lift."

They set the bar back in place on the door of the cave room. They crept to the west door of the hall. They slid back the bar inch by inch, so that it made no sound. Inch by inch, they pulled the door open. Out into the fresh night air they crept. Inch by inch, they pushed the door shut.

At the edge of the lake they bound their strong skates to their feet. Then Ross the Finn took Prince Harald's right hand in his own left hand, and side by side, the small dark Finn and the small fair prince began to skate south by night to Ordland.

8. HOW PRINCE HARALD
WENT TO KING ERIC

Over the ice, under a black sky full of sharp silver stars, sped little prince Harald and Ross the Finn. The boy put up his head to sniff the fresh night air.

"The air is mild for yuletide," he said. "Will the ice hold, do you think?"

"Oh yes, the wind is mild, but not mild enough to bring a thaw," said Ross the Finn. "All the same, we must be careful as we skirt the foot of Haki's grave mound."

"Why?" asked little prince Harald.

"Haki's grave mound looks over the Place of the Cattle Branding," said Ross the Finn. "And that's where the thaw will set in first."

"Why?" asked the small prince again.

"At the cattle branding, cattle dung fell on the ice," said Ross the Finn. "It eats its way into the ice, making it soft and weak. Ah, did you not feel the ice give then under your skate?"

"A little," said Prince Harald. "It was just here, then, that you and I first met, Ross, just under Haki's grave. Then the ice was full of men and cattle, and the air was full of the blare of bulls and the shouts of cowherds. Now only you and I are here, and the air is as still as the grave – as Haki's grave."

Ross the Finn gave a slight shiver.

"Why are you shivering?" asked the little prince. "Are you cold?"

"No," said Ross the Finn. "But you know that all Finns are a little troll-wise, and troll-wise men can see some things that will happen. And when you said the air was as still as the grave, I saw that this Place of the Cattle Branding was soon to be a grave."

"So long as it is not yours or mine," said Prince Harald. "If you are troll-wise, Ross, then you knew all the time who took the yule feast from my father's table?"

"I knew, but it was not mine to tell him," said Ross the Finn.

"Can you tell me?" the little prince asked.

"I can tell you, because when you next sit at a table, you will eat that feast," said Ross. "It was King Eric the Merry."

"But why did he take it?" asked Prince Harald. "Is he so poor that he had no yule feast of his own?"

"King Eric is not as rich as your father," said Ross the Finn. "His hall has no golden roof. Nor is he so poor that he has need of any other king's yule feast. He took your father's feast, my prince, to draw you to him by a kind of magic afterwards."

"He wants me to go to him?" cried Prince Harald. "Then why did you not tell me? And why did he not send for me?"

"If he is to help you, my prince," said Ross the Finn, "you had to want to go to him."

"To help me? In what way is King Eric to help me?" asked Prince Harald.

"You have a important fate," said Ross the Finn. "But it seems it is a fate you may well forget. King Eric can only help you to reach out to it if you come to his hall when you are ten years old."

"But how did he know I might not reach out to it?" asked Prince Harald. "He has never seen me, or I him."

"The birds that nest in his hall thatch have sung to tell him so," said Ross the Finn.

"If King Eric has such gifts," said the little prince, "why is he not rich? It seems to me he has it in his power to bend both men and things to his own ends."

"It is not his will to be rich," said Ross the Finn. "And he will never turn his troll gifts to self gain, but only to the good of others."

"Yet with all this," said Prince Harald, "men say no king is as merry."

"That is so," said Ross. "His is a merry hall, from dawn to dark."

"All his hall needs then," said Prince Harald, "is a prince of my own age for me to play with."

"It doesn't have a small prince, but it has a small princess," Ross told him. "She is the same age as you, she has red hair, like her father, she is lively and good, and her name is Princess Gyda."

"Oh, let's reach that hall soon!" cried Prince Harald. "How soon shall we reach it, Ross?"

"By dawn," said Ross the Finn. "By the sunset door we went out from King Alfdan's hall. By the sunrise door we will go into King Eric's."

On, on, as swift and as light as birds, they sped over the ice. The black sky grew less dark. The sharp stars faded.

Soon the sky began to grow pale. The shapes of the trees at the edge of the lake began to grow clear. And at last, in a gap in the line of the trees, they saw the big black bulk of a hall.

"Is that King Eric's hall?" asked Prince Harald.

"It is, my prince," said Ross the Finn. "You see, a ten-year-old prince can skate from Hadland to Ordland!"

The sun rose as they drew near. They saw the sunrise door, the east door of the hall, swing wide open. Out of it came a man, tall and big. With him came a small girl. Side by side they stood at the sunrise door, to greet the sun as it rose.

"Is that King Eric?" asked Prince Harald.

"It is," said Ross the Finn.

"Is that Princess Gyda with him?" asked Prince Harald.

"It is," said Ross the Finn.

"She stands with her father to greet the sun as I stand each dawn with mine," said Prince Harald. "Ross, if my father has not yet found that I have left his hall, he will find it out now, when I do not go to greet the sun with him."

They skated to the edge of the ice. It was midwinter, yet the birds in King Eric's hall thatch sang as loud and sweet to greet the sun as if it were spring.

Ross the Finn bent and took off his skates. Then up the bank of the lake he went to King Eric. Prince Harald did the same. He saw that King Eric was big and hearty with brown skin and red hair and beard. He saw how his red hair and his red beard blew about him in the wind. He saw how Princess Gyda's long red hair blew up to mix with King Eric's red beard.

"King Eric," said Ross the Finn, "I bring you Prince Harald of Hadland."

The eyes of the little prince met the eyes of the big king. Prince Harald saw that King Eric's eyes were merry. But he saw, too, that they had the look of eyes that saw more than other eyes saw.

"It is not Prince Harald of Hadland that you bring me," said King Eric, "but King Harald of Norway." Then he bent down, and took Prince Harald's small hand in his own big brown fist.

"I am glad for Norway's sake to see you, Harald Fairhair," he said. "So is Gyda, here, and so are the birds in my hall thatch. Gyda, take your guest in and wash his hands and feet. Give him something to eat and to drink, then let him sleep. When you have slept, Harald Fairhair, you shall help us to eat up your father's yule feast."

Princess Gyda shook back her long red hair. She put out her hand and took the hand of Prince Harald. She led him in by the sunrise door into King Eric's hall.

9. How His Uncle Went After Prince Harald

Just at the time when Princess Gyda led Prince Harald by the sunrise door into King Eric's hall, at the far end of the lake King Alfdan the Black went out by his own sunrise door. Queen Ragnild and Prince Guthorm went out with him, to greet the sun. But Prince Harald was not to be seen.

"Our Fairhair sleeps late today," said Prince Guthorm. "I will fetch him." That was Prince Guthorm's way of trying to shield the young prince from the black moods of King Alfdan.

Prince Guthorm was a grown man now, as brave as he was wise, and as wise as he was brave. He was so skillful with a sword that from the day he was sixteen years old, he had led King Alfdan's men.

In he went to Prince Harald's sleeping room. Prince Harald was not in his bed, he was not in his room, he was not in the hall. "It may be that he went out to groom his horse," said Prince Guthorm. And out he went, to seek him in the stable.

By the dim dawn light, as he went, he saw footprints in the snow. Two sets ran side by side. He saw that they were the prints of a boy and of a man, small and slight of frame.

He saw that they came from the sunset door of the hall. So he went to it, and tried it. At his light push, it swung open.

He went back to track the footprints. From the sunset door, they led down to the edge of the lake. At the edge of the ice they came to an end, but at that same spot skate marks began, two sets that ran south side by side. They were fresh, made since last sunset.

He saw that they ran to the Place of the Cattle Branding. But all the way to the foot of Haki's grave mound, the vast sheet of blue-white ice was bare. No small prince and no small slight man were to be seen on the ice.

Prince Guthorm went back and told all this to King Alfdan. King Alfdan's looks grew black. "Two sets of skate marks?" he cried. "Find out who went with the lad!"

Prince Guthorm put his horn to his lips, and blew the note for the roll call. At the sound, his men ran and fell in, rank on rank. There were no gaps in the ranks.

"Is the hall just as it was left last night?" asked Prince Guthorm.

His right-hand man told him, "Lord, the table is missing one dish, one ale horn, and one meat dagger."

"Did anyone wake in the night?" asked Prince Guthorm. "Did anyone hear any noise in the hall?" But no one had.

"Lord," said his right-hand man again, "well-fed men sleep deep."

"But hungry men don't," said Prince Guthorm. "So maybe Ross the Finn can tell us more." He strode up the hall to the door of the cave room. He cried in a tone that rang along the roof, "Ross, did you hear men in the hall in the night?"

Each man in the hall held his breath. It was so still in the hall that even the stir of a foot on straw echoed loudly. But no sound came from the dark cave room.

Prince Guthorm slid back the bar of the door of the cave room. He flung the door wide open. "Ross!" he cried again. "Did you hear men in the hall in the night?"

But still no sound came from the dark cave room. Prince Guthorm bent to stare into the gloom, "Saxo, bring me a torch!" he said to his right-hand man.

Saxo ran to light a pine torch and to bring it to Prince Guthorm. By its red glow, the prince saw the bindings that had tied Ross the Finn's hands and feet. They lay, cut, on the floor. By them lay a dish, an ale horn, and a meat dagger. Apart from them, the cave room was bare.

The news flew from lip to lip down the hall: "Ross the Finn has fled! It is with Ross the Finn that our small Fairhair has fled!"

The eyes of King Alfdan were flashing with rage as they met the eyes of Prince Guthorm. "So it was to steal my son from me," he cried, "that the Finn came to my hall!"

"It could be," said Prince Guthorm, "that our Fairhair went with him of his own free will."

"I don't care if he did," cried King Alfdan the Black. "Take men, Guthorm, and track them, and bring them both back to me!"

So Guthorm and a band of the king's men set out on sledges to track the skate marks on the ice. Each sledge was drawn by three strong horses.

Clip-clop, clip-clop, as swift as birds over the ice they went. On and on the tracks led them, till they came to the foot of Haki's grave mound.

Then Prince Guthorm held back his horses, and held his hand high, to tell his men to halt.

"But the tracks go on, lord," said Saxo.

"They do," said Prince Guthorm. "But do you not see

how soft and weak the ice is in the Place of the Cattle Branding?"

"It held under the skates," said Saxo.

"Ice that holds under skates may not hold under sledges," said Prince Guthorm. "We must skirt this weak ice and pick up the skate tracks again when we are past it."

So round the edge of the weak ice went each sledge, to pick up the skate tracks again on the far side of the Place of the Cattle Branding.

Clip-clop, clip-clop, swift as birds they went on. The tracks led them to the south end of the lake till they saw, in a gap in the trees, a hall with a deep thatch of straw.

"We must be on Ordland ice now," said Prince Guthorm to Saxo. "From the straw thatch, I take that to be the hall of King Eric of Ordland."

They saw that the skate marks came to an end at the edge of the lake below King Eric's hall. From the lake they saw two sets of footprints go up the snow of the bank to the sunrise door of the hall. Like the footprints that had led down to the lake from King Alfdan's sunset door, they were the prints of a boy and of a man, small and slight of frame.

"So our Fairhair fled to King Eric the Merry!" cried Saxo. "Why did he do something so odd and so bold?"

"This thing must go deeper than just a small lad's prank," said Prince Guthorm. "I think we shall find the hand of fate in it."

Prince Guthorm left his sledge and went up from the edge of the lake to the hall. The birds in the hall thatch sang loud as he blew a blast on the guest horn.

The door of the hall swung wide open. Men came out to meet and greet him. Into the hall and up to the high seat was Prince Guthorm led with joy.

On his high seat sat King Eric, big and brown. On two stools at his feet sat little princess Gyda and little prince Harald. Red head and fair head were bent over chessmen of gold and of silver. King Eric's red bush of a beard swept over fair head and red head as he bent to help each child in turn. That red beard shook with laughter as King Eric made joke after joke. The little prince and princess shook with laughter, too. All the hall was loud with the laughter of King Eric's men.

It did Prince Guthorm good to see the face of little prince Harald so bright and lively. But Prince Harald's bright face fell when Prince Guthorm told King Eric he had been sent to take his nephew back.

"It is not my will to go back yet, Uncle Guthorm. King Eric is a merry host, I enjoy being his guest. And Gyda is the best friend I ever had."

King Eric gave a merry shrug. "If he will not go with you of his own free will, Prince Guthorm," he said, "I can't let him go at all. For he is my guest, and the guest law must be kept."

"And Ross the Finn, King Eric?"

"He, too, is my guest, and the guest law must be kept," said King Eric. "But stay today and tonight with us, and help us eat and drink King Alfdan's yule feast. At dawn you shall go back and beg King Alfdan for me to let his son stay here in Ordland till the spring."

Prince Guthorm was glad to stay that day and that night. It was long since he had spent time in a hall so full of lively cheer. Joke for joke he gave back, to top the jokes of King Eric. The hall rang with men's laughter. Each time, Prince Harald's face lit up, and Princess Gyda shook back her long red hair to smile at him.

"Harald Fairhair," Gyda said, "I like your uncle a lot, as you like my father. I will share my father with you, if you will share your uncle with me."

"Let's shake hands on that!" cried the little prince, and took her hand in his. "Now your father shall be my father, and my uncle shall be your uncle, as long as we all live."

"What if it is not my will?" asked Prince Guthorm, with a twinkle.

"Oh, but it is your will, Uncle Guthorm!" cried Princess Gyda.

"The birds in my hall thatch sing that it is fate's will," said King Eric. "Yet it is still up to each person whether they follow fate's will or not."

"Will our Fairhair follow fate's will, do you think?"

"With Gyda to urge him on, I think he will," said King Eric. "If so, this little lad who pulls this little girl's hair will be the first king of all Norway."

"How will so vast a thing come to pass?" Prince Guthorm asked.

"So important a fate can only come from much pain," said King Eric. "All except for three small parts of Norway must be won with bloodshed."

"And those three parts?" asked Prince Guthorm.

"Hadland, Ringrik, and Ordland," King Eric told him. "Hadland is his by birth. Ringrik is his by your gift. Ordland will be his by my gift. But that will not be till all the rest is won."

"My gift to start, your gift to end," said Prince Guthorm.

"And all the rest, the pain and clang of battle, as my birds sing," King Eric said.

10. How Haki's Death Wish Came True

Next day, Prince Guthorm was up at dawn. With King Eric, Prince Harald, and Princess Gyda, he went out by the sunrise door to greet the sun.

Then down the snowbank to the edge of the lake they went to the sledges. Prince Harald ran to help Saxo hold back the horses of the first sledge as Prince Guthorm got into it. Princess Gyda ran to tuck his furs about him.

"Take care that the ice holds, Uncle Guthorm," said Prince Harald.

"Yes, Uncle Guthorm, take care that the ice holds," said Princess Gyda.

"When Ross and I came past Haki's grave mound," said the prince, "Ross saw with troll-sight that the Place of the Cattle Branding will soon be a grave."

"And not only Ross," said King Eric. "For the birds in my hall thatch sing that the breath of death creeps from Haki's grave mound. Take care."

"I will take care," said Prince Guthorm with a smile.

Then off over the ice went his sledge. Clip-clop, clip-clop, rang the hoofs of his horses on the ice. And he went back to Hadland with the king's men.

When Haki's grave mound came in sight, they took care to skirt the soft, weak ice in the Place of the Cattle Branding. So all came back safe and sound to the hall with the golden roof.

When Prince Guthorm came up from the lake and into the hall, King Alfdan had just begun to twist a new bowstring for his bow. He saw Prince Guthorm come in, no Finn and no small prince with him. His eyebrows drew into a black frown, and so hard did he pull the bowstring that its snapping sang down the hall like a harp string.

Prince Guthorm told him how he had found the little prince with King Eric, safe and well and lively. "And King Eric begs you will let our Fairhair stay with him till spring," he said.

With a face as black as a thundercloud, King Alfdan threw down his bow and strode down his hall. "Get out my sledge!" he cried to his men. "If my son will not come when I send for him, I will go and fetch him myself."

"I beg you to let him stay, Alfdan," said Prince Guthorm. "It is good for a lad of his age to see new lands and new ways."

"You are too soft with him, Guthorm," said King Alfdan. "I myself will fetch him back."

"Lord," said Torlef the Wise, "I too beg you not to go."

King Alfdan swung around on his wise man. "You, too, Torlef?" he cried. "Are you and Guthorm against me together?"

"Lord," said Torlef, "Prince Guthorm begs you for Prince Harald's sake. I beg you for your own. Think, lord – how old are you?"

"I am forty winters old, as you well know," said King Alfdan. "But why are you asking that now?"

"Forty winters old," said Torlef, "was Haki the Wolf's Head when he died on the ice. Do you not remember the death wish he cried on you then?"

"If you do not, Alfdan, I do," said Prince Guthorm. "This is what Haki cried in his death hour: 'You have won Princess Ragnild, Alfdan the Black. But when you reach the age that I am now, take heed, in case the ice brings you to your death as now it brings me to mine.'"

"I wasn't afraid of Haki in the flesh," cried the king, "and I'm less afraid of Haki dead. I will go to Ordland this very day."

"Alfdan!" cried Queen Ragnild. "Do not tempt a dead man's death wish. Let Harald stay with King Eric till spring. Then we can all go by boat to fetch him back. Do not risk the ice when the wind is so mild it may well bring a thaw."

"No thaw has set in yet," said King Alfdan. "Today I will go to Ordland."

And out he went, and down the snowbank to his sledge. Prince Guthorm went with him down to the edge of the lake. "It is true that no thaw has set in yet, Alfdan," he said. "But keep clear of the Place of the Cattle Branding. At the foot of Haki's grave mound, the ice is weak and soft, and Ross the Finn saw with troll-sight that it is soon to be a grave."

"Don't tell me about the Finn!" cried King Alfdan. "Wasn't it he who took my son away?"

He was so angry when he set off that he didn't listen to what Prince Guthorm had said, but drove his horses hard due south for Ordland. His whip sent his horses on far ahead of the rest of the sledges. His sledge sped on alone. And alone he came to the Place of the Cattle Branding.

He was so angry that he didn't pay attention to the ice.

He did not see, as Prince Guthorm had seen, how the cattle dung had sunk in and made the ice soft and weak. He did not see how the marks of Prince Guthorm's sledges went round on the solid ice. He saw only that the track of the skates carried on.

And on he went after them.

With the loud clip-clop of his horses in his ears, he did not hear the ice crack. Too late to pull up his horses in time, he saw a black pit yawn in the blue-white ice. He felt the sledge keel over and he shot down into a deep black pit of ice-cold water.

The horses began to thrash and to rear up in the water, seeking for a firm foothold. Under the ice they went and under the ice with them they pulled King Alfdan the Black.

The other sledges pulled up at the edge of the Place of the Cattle Branding. Each man left his sledge and crept on hands and knees to the rim of the black pit.

"I will go in after him," said Saxo. "Tie a lifeline to my belt, and pull in hard when I tug it." They tied a lifeline to Saxo's belt, and held it tight. Into the water he went, and they saw the deep black water close over his head.

They felt him tug. They pulled the line in, and when he came up, he had King Alfdan lifeless in his arms. They took the dead king from him and pulled Saxo on to the ice.

The men carried the dead king back to the sledges, at the foot of Haki's grave mound. They carried Saxo too, limp but still alive. Then they sped back to the hall with the golden roof.

Sad and slow rang the steps of the men as they carried the dead king up the long hall, and laid him at the feet of Queen Ragnild.

Queen Ragnild knelt and wept over him as, with white hands, she smoothed his wet black hair. But Torlef the Wise stood with grave face and bit his lip, his hand on his beard, for he saw the rocks and the reefs that lay ahead.

He said to Prince Guthorm, "Prince Harald must come back now. But your place is with the queen, she will need you in her loss. So this time it is I who must go and bring our small king home." And so the sledges sped over the ice one again to Ordland.

As he reached the edge of the lake, Torlef the Wise saw King Eric come to the door of his hall. He stood in the snow, as still as a stout brown tree, to catch the sound of the song the birds sang so loud in his hall thatch.

Torlef walked up the snowbank to him. He told him everything that had happened.

"Your Fairhair and my Gyda went up to the hills, to ski with Ross the Finn," King Eric said. "I will send men to bring him to you. For now, come in and eat."

As they sat at the table, Torlef said, "See how the king's anger made Haki's evil death wish come true! And see now what ill fate it brings for Hadland and Ringrik. A strong king has died in his prime, and he has left his lands to a boy only ten years old!"

"Yet, with you and Queen Ragnild and Prince Guthorm to teach him how to rule," said King Eric, "even so small a lad can be a strong king too."

"It is the king's men, lord, who will not want so small a lad as their king," said Torlef. "If Prince Guthorm will take it, the crown of both lands is his."

King Eric sat with his big red beard in his big fist. "I think that may be his men's will, but not his," said King Eric. "For it is his own wish to help the dream in the pigsty to come true. And Harold Fairhair must first be king of his own two small lands if he is to end up as king of all Norway."

"Do you think this will happen?" asked Torlef.

"It was a fate he might well have forgotten," said King Eric, "had he not met my Gyda. But my child has red hair, Torlef. She will urge him to reach out to what fate wants for him, if he wants it, too. That's why I made my plans for them to meet this yuletide. That, Torlef, is why you're now eating King Alfdan's yuletide feast."

Then Torlef saw Ross the Finn come into the hall. And

with him, hand in hand, eyes bright and cheeks aglow, came little prince Harald and little princess Gyda.

Torlef told Prince Harald about his father's death. Prince Harald laid his small hand in the big fist of King Eric. "I must go back to my mother, she will need me," he said.

Then he threw out his arms and gave Gyda a big hug. "I'll never forget you, Gyda," he said. "See that you don't forget me. As soon as I'm old enough to marry, I shall send for you to come and be my bride."

Gyda gave a toss of her red head. "The man I marry," said she, "must be king of more than two small lands!"

"What must he be king of?" asked Prince Harald.

"All of Norway," said the princess.

"Then that I will be!" said the prince. And back he went with Torlef, to the hall with the golden roof.

11. How the Dream in the Pigsty Came True

Queen Ragnild was glad when her son came home, and so was his uncle, Prince Guthorm. But the king's men stood back, and gave the lad cold looks.

"Be honest with me, Prince Guthorm," said Torlef the Wise. "If your men want it, will you take the crown?"

"I don't want it," said Prince Guthorm. "And if my men want it, they won't want it for long."

That night, as his men lay down to sleep, he said to them, "It will soon be the day when we take Prince Harald as our king. Let each of you rub his helmet and shield and coat of mail bright, to match the new gold arm rings he will give you on that day."

He saw how each man's face grew dark at this. Each man began to growl in his beard.

"A lad ten winters old is no king for us, lord," said Saxo.

The next man said, "We need a grown man for a king, lord, wise in the ways of war, and with skill in swordcraft."

Then all the men gave a shout. "We need you, lord! We want you, Prince Guthorm, as our king!"

Prince Guthorm's eyes went from face to face. His own face was stern. He stood still, and did not speak.

"Lord, the land of Ringrik is your land by right," cried Saxo. "When your father, King Sigurd the Hart, was killed, you were as small a lad as Prince Harald is now. So you did not take it then. Now the time is right for you to do so."

"Men!" cried Prince Guthorm. "All of you sat in this hall when Ragnild my sister married King Alfdan. Do you remember what I said then? If you cannot tell me, I will tell you."

Then Saxo said, "Lord, you said this: 'The land of Ringrik will be mine. But I vow never to be its king. I give it to you, Alfdan and Ragnild, to add to your own land of Hadland. For it seems to me that when two small lands each have a king, both lands are weak. But when two small lands have the same king, both lands are strong.'"

"That vow I have kept," said Prince Guthorm. "That vow I will keep. Take our Fairhair as king of both lands, and you will find he has an important fate in store. As for the lad's age, that is a thing time will soon cure."

"And till then, lord?" asked Saxo.

And Prince Guthorm told the men, "Till then, Queen Ragnild and Lord Torlef will rule for him in things of state and teach him statecraft. I will lead his men as I led his father's, and we, his men, will teach him swordcraft and the ways of war. Men, I think that out of this small lad we shall make a strong king!"

At that, a cheer went up from the men. "On such terms, lord," they cried, "we will take our Fairhair as king!"

So, on the day set by Torlef, little prince Harald sat in his father's high seat. And one by one his men came up the long hall to him, and put a big hand in his small hands, and took him to be their king.

Bright was the hall with gold cloth that day. Bright shone each helmet, each shield, each coat of mail, and the gold arm rings that the new king gave his men that day. And the feast was rich that night. The men sat at the long table, and ate and drank and made merry.

Now the slow years went by, and King Harald Fairhair grew up. Everything went well all this time with his two small lands of Hadland and Ringrik. Yet this was no thanks to him, for he left it to others to rule them. Nor did he show any wish to add other lands to his own.

As time went on in this way, his men said to each other, "Is this the strong king, wise in the ways of war, we were to have? This is no king, but a weakling who mopes in the hall from dawn to dusk."

And Queen Ragnild said to herself with a sigh, "When will this small thorn, that my son is still, grow into the vast tree of my dream?"

And even Torlef the Wise shook his head, and said to Prince Guthorm, "Wasn't Harald Fairhair born to do more than this, to be more than this? The years go by, yet he doesn't lift a hand to make the dream in the pigsty come true!"

"Put your trust in King Eric, Torlef," said Prince Guthorm. "Didn't he say Princess Gyda would urge our Fairhair to stretch out his hand to his fate? We shall see that in due time he will do this."

So the time came when King Harald was old enough to get married. He sent for his uncle, Prince Guthorm. He sent for his wise man, Torlef. He told them, "When I was ten winters old, I chose Princess Gyda of Ordland to be my bride. Go now to her father, King Eric, and ask him for her hand for me."

Prince Guthorm and Torlef the Wise took a band of the king's men. They took a ship with red ropes and with sails of blue and white silk. And in this they went south down the lake to the hall of King Eric of Ordland.

King Eric was still big and stout and brown and merry. His red head and his red beard still didn't have a single white hair. When they told him why they came, his red beard began to shake with laughter.

"He sent you to ask *me* for her hand?" he cried. "Never tell Gyda that! Her hair is red, as you well know, and she is apt to flare up like a pine torch! She is a girl with a mind of her own, a girl with a will of her own. Let us find out that mind now."

He led them up the stone stairs that went from the hall to her room. In her room, Princess Gyda sat at a silver loom, and weaving bright gold cloth. Her hair, as she bent to the loom, was like a wave of flame. Her silver shuttle flew to and fro. From edge to edge of the cloth it drew the gold thread with a flash like that of a spear.

She rose as they came in, and they saw that she was as tall and as swift and as strong as a spear herself. "Uncle Guthorm!" she cried. And she came to him and took both his hands in hers. "Is it to see my father or is it to see me that you come after so many years?" she asked.

Just in time, Prince Guthorm saw the twinkle in King Eric's eye. "To see you, Gyda," he said. "Do you remember how, when you were ten years old, Harald Fairhair told you of his wish to marry you? Now you are both old enough to marry, and he sends me to ask you if you will be his bride."

She lifted up her bright head and shook her red hair back, in the same way she had as a child. "You were not with us, Uncle Guthorm," she said, "but Lord Torlef was. So he knows, if you do not, that I told Harald Fairhair not to send for me till he ruled over all of Norway. Now both of you go back, and tell him that again."

"But stay and eat first," said King Eric.

As the three men sat at the table, he said, "My red Gyda has the fire that Harald Fairhair lacks. Fire he needs if he is to reach out to grasp his fate. Tell him from me that when he has won the rest of Norway, Ordland shall be my wedding gift to him."

So, in the ship with red ropes and with blue and white silk sails, Prince Guthorm and Torlef the Wise went north up the lake to the hall with the golden roof. "Do you think he will flare into red rage when we tell him?" Torlef asked Prince Guthorm. "Or fall into a black mood, like his father?"

"I do not know," said Prince Guthorm. "He is my own sister's son, yet I feel that much must lie deep in him that I have not yet seen."

So they came to King Harald and told him, "Princess asked us to tell you she will not marry you till you rule all of Norway."

King Harald did not flare into red rage. Nor did he fall into a black mood, like his father. He sat still for a time on his high seat, his flax-pale head on his hand. Then he said, "I owe Gyda thanks. For she reminds me of important things. Here and now I make this vow: that I will not clip or cut my hair till I rule all the land of Norway."

Then Torlef was glad that Gyda had urged Harald to reach out to grasp his fate. And Queen Ragnild was glad to see the small thorn of her dream start to grow at last. And Prince Guthorm cried, for his own self and for all the king's men, "Harald, it is with joy we hear you vow such a kingly vow!"

From that day, King Harald Fairhair let his fair hair grow. He did not clip it, he did not cut it. It grew so fast and so

long that the time came when his flax-pale locks were as long as Gyda's red ones. It grew so fast and so long that the time came when his flax-pale locks were as long as the long fair lock in King Alfdan's dream.

And now, just to see this man with his long pale hair, at the head of his men, struck fear into his enemies. For as his hair grew in length, he grew in strength, and in skill, and in wisdom. He grew wise in the ways of men and of wars. He grew in skill in swordcraft and statecraft. He grew into a strong king.

With Prince Guthorm he led out the men of Hadland and Ringrik to win land after land. In battle after battle the swords sang and the spears thundered. In battle after battle, coats of mail were pierced and shields were bent and helmets broken, and blades grew hot, and fields grew red.

As in Queen Ragnild's dream, the roots of the tree that was King Harald were roots as red as blood.

There were many roots that had to be torn up so that King Harald's might be firm and strong. Many kings and many men fell in battle. Many came to King Harald, to be his men. Many who held to the old ways had to escape from Norway, to start a new life in distant lands. Others escaped to sea and, as Vikings, set sail in longships to rob and to raid other lands.

After three years, King Harald Fairhair was the only free king, save one, left in all Norway. The other free king was King Eric the Merry of Ordland.

King Harald Fairhair came back to his hall with its golden roof. He cut his long locks short and he sent for Prince Guthorm and Torlef the Wise.

He said to them, "Go again to Princess Gyda. Tell her that now I rule all of Norway."

So once again Prince Guthorm and Torlef took a band of the king's men. Again they took a ship with red ropes and sails of blue and white silk, and they went south down the lake to the hall of King Eric of Ordland.

It was with great gladness that Princess Gyda went back with them, with her hair blowing in the wind like locks of flame. Gladly, too, went King Eric, big and stout and brown and merry, his red beard blowing this way and that as he stood in the prow of the ship.

And with all gladness King Harald and Queen Ragnild met them. The wedding feast was rich and merry. And King Eric gladly kept his vow, and gave to King Harald his own small land of Ordland as a wedding gift.

This was the start of many years of joy and plenty, the years that in Queen Ragnild's dream were the trunk of the tree as green as grass. All the land of Norway was at peace. The crops grew ripe. The barns were full.

When at last King Harald Fairhair died, he was eighty-three years old. His flax-pale locks had, for many years, been as white as snow, as white as the twigs on the tree in Queen Ragnild's dream.

This was how Harald Fairhair came to be the first king to rule over all of Norway. And so Queen Ragnild's dream, and the dream in the pigsty, came true.

ABOUT THIS BOOK

The stories in this book are based on stories and legends from several ancient sources:

History of the Danish Kings, by Saxo Grammaticus (twelfth century)

The Ragnar Cycle, in the *Elder Edda* (twelfth century)

Saga of Ragnar Lodbroc and his Sons, Icelandic saga (thirteenth century)

Faroese Ragnar-Ballads (fourteenth century)

'King Ragnar's Death Song' from *Kraku-mal,* in the *Elder Edda* (twelfth century)

Asla is the name of King Ragnar's queen in the Faroese version. In the Danish and Icelandic versions, she is Aslaug.

In the Faroe Isles, the fourteenth century ballads of Sigurd and Ragnar were (and still are) sung for dancing on the long winter evenings from Christmas to Lent. The leader of the dance sings the story, stanza by stanza, and in between the stanzas the rest of the dancers sing a chorus. The verse that King Ragnar sings in Chapters 6 and 8 is based on the chorus of the Ragnar ballard.